A Cornish
GIFT

A Cornish
GIFT

Fern
Britton

HarperCollins*Publishers*

HarperCollins*Publishers*
The News Building
1 London Bridge Street,
London SE1 9GF

www.harpercollins.co.uk

Published by HarperCollins*Publishers* 2017
1

First Published in Great Britain by HarperCollins*Publishers* 2014, 2015

A catalogue record for this book is available from the British Library

ISBN: 978-0-00-825310-3

Set in Birka by Palimpsest Book Production Limited, Falkirk, Stirlingshire

Printed and bound by CPI Group (UK) Ltd, Croydon CR0 4YY

MIX
Paper from
responsible sources
FSC™ C007454

This book is produced from independently certified FSC™ paper
to ensure responsible forest management.

For more information visit: www.harpercollins.co.uk/green

A Cornish
CAROL

1

'Darling!' Helen dashed out of Gull's Cry and threw her arms around her daughter-in-law Terri as she headed up the path to the cottage door. Sean, Helen's son, was behind her, carrying their daughter, Summer, in her car seat.

Summer's chubby face split into the sunniest of smiles as she saw Helen. 'Gan Gan!' she cried joyfully and reached out her little hands for a cuddle.

'I can't believe how much you've grown!' Helen exclaimed. 'And is that a new tooth I can see?'

'Yes, and it's unbelievable the trouble that one tiny tooth has caused,' said Sean as they headed indoors.

He placed the car seat on the floor and started to undo the clasp that held Summer safely in place. The moment her granddaughter was free, Helen swept her up and showered her with kisses, which were returned enthusiastically.

This done, and after more hugs and kisses all round, they made their way into Helen's cosy sitting room, where Sean and Terri sank into the comfy armchairs with relief. The tell-tale signs of disturbed nights and fraught days were all too obvious to Helen as she took in the dark circles under their eyes.

'Teething can be a rotten old business for everyone,' she concurred, gently stroking Summer's flushed cheeks. 'Well, the good news is that Granny is here to take some of the strain. This Christmas, the only things you'll need to worry about are eating, drinking and making merry. We've got Piran on chef duty – he's a much better cook than me and he can't bear having me in the kitchen with him, which means I'll have more time to spend on you three.'

'You have no idea how good that sounds,' said Terri, gratefully. 'The cottage looks amazing by the way.'

'Thank you,' Helen preened.

Interior design was a passion of hers and she

had lovingly devoted the last few days to making sure that her cottage really looked the part this year. The windows and doorway were wreathed in branches of fir adorned with twinkling lights, while giant candles flickered in storm lanterns on the window ledges. The banisters and mantelpiece were decorated with more fir branches and holly, and there were beautiful handcrafted wicker reindeer dotted around the room. Taking centre stage, the tree by the fireplace was utterly gorgeous; decorated sparingly with hand-painted sea-glass decorations that twinkled and cast dancing reflections of the crackling fire in the stove. The combination of fairy lights and candles gave the room a warm ambient glow, and the aroma of pine mingled with oranges and cloves scented the air.

'It's absolutely heavenly,' sighed Terri, sinking deep into the armchair.

Tempting as it was to lean back and enjoy the chance to relax, Sean forced himself to his feet. 'I'll just grab the last of the bags and then I'll be ready for one of your legendary winter warmers, Mum.'

'I've added a dash of sloe gin to the mulled

wine this year and I've got some mince pies warming in the oven – not home-made, I'm afraid, but they are from the new artisan bakery in Trevay and they're scrummy.'

'Amazing.' Sean gave his Mum a peck on the cheek and set off to get the rest of their luggage.

'You're all in the big bedroom!' she shouted after him.

'But that's your bedroom,' Terri protested.

'It's got more space and Piran and I will be quite happy in the little one, it'll be very cosy.'

'How is Piran?'

'Oh, you know.' Helen smiled ruefully, thinking about her grumpy, difficult, enigmatic, yet oh-so-magnetic boyfriend. They had chosen not to live together, both valuing their independence. He could be infuriating and unreadable but at the same time generous, exciting and sometimes completely magnificent. Lately, however . . . Helen couldn't put her finger on it, but he'd been far more withdrawn and brooding than usual. Probably the full moon, she told herself. Nothing to worry about – yet . . .

Helen checked her watch. It was gone five o'clock.

'Hope you both fancy a good laugh tonight. We've got tickets for the local am-dram panto – they're doing *Aladdin*.'

Sean struggled in with the luggage. 'Oh, great. All wobbly sets and fluffed lines as usual?'

Helen laughed. 'Guaranteed! I wouldn't miss it for the world!'

*

It was a packed house at the church hall. There were only three performances of the panto and tonight's would be the last. Helen's best friend, Penny, had landed the plum role of Aladdin. Penny was a hotshot TV producer and owner of Penny Leighton Productions, best known for her worldwide success with the *Mr Tibbs Mysteries* series and for her work on the Oscar-nominated film *Hats Off, Trevay!*. Helen knew that Penny would rather be chewing her own arm off than getting sucked into yet more village bother, but she also knew that Penny took her role of vicar's wife very seriously indeed and that meant supporting the panto, all proceeds of which went to support the church's charitable work.

Also wanting to do his bit, Simon Canter, Penny's husband and the father of their daughter Jenna, had gamely taken on the role of Widow Twanky. Much as she adored him, Helen couldn't help but feel that Simon had been hopelessly miscast. He was a wonderful person – kind, decent and a thoroughly good egg – but there was no denying that he lacked the requisite bawdy humour essential for making the part sing. The topical jokes he'd been given about Kim Kardashian's bum and 'twerking' had fallen flat in the first act. And watching him now, holding two melons and doing a 'nudge nudge, wink, wink' over a 'lovely pair' was quite painful. It was hard to escape the thought that this was all rather inappropriate behaviour for a vicar. Penny was doing her best to carry the show, but she was far above her material, Helen thought.

Sean had opted to stay at home with Summer, who was a bit grizzly, so Helen had ended up sitting between Terri and Piran. A happy and animated Jenna was bouncing on her knee, shouting out loudly and eagerly every time her mummy and daddy came on stage.

Helen risked a glance at Piran from the corner of her eye. He'd barely said a word all evening, except to ask them what they wanted to drink during the interval, returning with plastic cups of orange squash. While everyone around them was laughing at the antics on stage, Piran's head was lowered and his piercing blue eyes stared disdainfully from hooded eyelids. His hand covered his mouth as if trying to stop angry words from escaping and he jiggled his leg impatiently. Clearly, his mood had not improved. Helen sighed and turned back to the performance.

Aladdin and Princess Lotus Blossom – who was being played by Lauren, one of the village girls – were making their escape on a magic carpet while murdering, or at least committing grievous bodily harm on 'Up Where We Belong', accompanied by the children of Pendruggan Juniors, who were pretending to be a flock of birds. What might have looked good on paper was somewhat let down by the execution. Firstly, the 'flying' carpet was supposed to appear suspended mid-air, not draped across one of the trestle tables normally reserved for serving biscuits and tea at church coffee mornings. Lauren was a well-fed lass and when she began giving it her all and belting out the lyrics, the table became decidedly unsteady. Secondly, the children shuffling onstage weren't quite progressing with military precision. Some were standing around looking bewildered, a couple of little boys were gurning at each other, and one little girl broke off and wandered to the front of the stage to tell her mummy she needed a wee-wee.

While the audience stifled their laughter, Aladdin and Princess Lotus Blossom continued gamely emoting about eagles crying on a mountain high, but their dirge was finally cut short when the shaky table leg gave way. Titters tuned to guffaws as Princess Lotus Blossom went arse over tit and ended up on her bottom, skirts in the air, with her frilly pink thong on show.

Tears of laughter streaming down her face, it was all Helen could do to hold on to Jenna, who was on her feet, screeching enthusiastically at the sight of her mummy rushing to help Lauren to recover whatever was left of her dignity. Rocking with mirth, Helen turned to say something to Piran, but the words died on her lips as she saw his stony face, eyes dark with displeasure.

*

'Well, that went off really well!' said Simon, happily supping at his post-panto pint of ale in the comfort of The Dolphin's cosy saloon bar and seemingly oblivious to the general consensus that this would go down as one of the most shambolic village pantos in living memory.

Penny turned to her husband, incredulous. 'Were you performing in the same play as the rest of us?'

Simon's good humour wasn't to be dented. 'I'd say it was at least as good as last year's *Jack and the Beanstalk*. Arguably, that was a lot worse. Don't you remember?'

'Oh, yes.' Penny shuddered at the memory of Queenie, who'd been playing Old Mother Hubbard, setting fire to the stage curtain while having a sneaky fag in the wings.

'Exactly! And we've raised over a thousand pounds from the box office, which will certainly go a long way to help with the funds for the trip to Canterbury Cathedral at Easter.'

'That's what I love about you, Simon – you're always able to see the positives in everything.' Penny gave her ruddy-cheeked, balding and bespectacled husband a loving kiss on his nose.

Helen couldn't help smiling at the display of affection. It was just the four of them in the pub; Terri had gone home to relieve Sean of babysitting duties, and little Jenna had fallen asleep, exhausted, and been carried home by Penny's brother, who'd come down with his family for the holidays.

'You're very quiet, Piran,' said Simon. 'How did you rate the performance this year?'

Piran kept his morose gaze firmly on his pint. 'No comment.'

'Not tempted to sign yourself up for next year?' Simon added playfully. 'Perhaps we could put on *Peter Pan* and you could play Captain Hook. You've got the perfect temperament for it and everyone loves a baddie!'

Piran glowered. 'Is that supposed to be a compliment?'

'No, no, I just meant—'

'I know what you meant!' Piran snapped. 'We haven't all got the urge to prance around like bloody fools for the merriment of others. Some of us have better things to do.'

Helen was shocked at the sharpness of his tone. 'Simon was only having a bit of fun, Piran.'

This earned her a fierce scowl, too, then, muttering darkly under his breath, Piran pushed his chair back and stalked off to the bar to buy another drink.

'Perhaps Prince Charming would be a better fit?' Helen said to his retreating back.

'I heard that *Beauty and the Beast* were casting.' Penny gave her friend a wry smile.

At this point, Audrey Tipton, the village busybody – a woman Helen always thought of as the love-child of Margaret Thatcher and Mussolini – came striding into the pub, with her husband Geoffrey, otherwise known as Mr Audrey Tipton, trotting along in her wake. Spotting Simon, Audrey held up a finger to her husband, as if commanding a dog to stay, then made a beeline for their table while Geoffrey hovered timidly by the pub entrance.

'Ah, Reverend Canter. I'm glad I found you.'

The sight of Audrey crossing The Dolphin's threshold had everyone's jaws dropping. She wouldn't normally be seen dead in anything quite so vulgar as a public house.

Simon got to his feet uncertainly. 'What can I do for you, Audrey? Would you and Geoff care for a drink?'

'No, thank you, Reverend,' she answered briskly. 'I'll make this as brief as possible. As you know, the Bridge Society Christmas luncheon was to have been held in the church hall tomorrow, but I've just been there and the hall is in a complete state of disarray. This really is quite unacceptable. If our annual luncheon suffers any disruption as a result, I shall hold you responsible.'

'Now, Audrey,' Simon's tone was conciliatory, 'you know that the panto has only just finished. I'm sure that Polly and all of the helpers are doing their best to get everything shipshape . . .'

'Well, their best clearly isn't good enough!'

'Give them a chance, Audrey!'

Over Audrey's shoulder, Helen caught sight of Piran returning from the bar. She was dismayed to see that the dangerous look in his

eye had taken on new fire as Audrey Tipton
delivered her rebuke. He and Audrey were
old adversaries, their hostility mutual and
frequently gladiatorial.

'Audrey.' Piran gave her a tight nod of the
head.

'Ah, Piran Ambrose. Pendruggan's answer to
Blackbeard!' Audrey turned to Simon again.
'Perhaps, Reverend, if you spent more time
attending to church matters and less time
frequenting drinking establishments with
undesirables, this sort of problem wouldn't
occur.'

'Now listen here—' Penny was on her feet,
ready to defend her husband, but before she
could say more, Piran placed his pint of
Cornish Knocker on the table and rounded
on Audrey.

Sensing what was coming, Helen put her
head in her hands. Of all the times for Audrey
to go rattling the bars of his cage . . .

'Now, Audrey, us undesirables don't care
much for what other people think,' said Piran,
his voice quiet but each word carefully enun-
ciated and delivered with venom. 'What's
more, we say what's on our minds. So here's

what I've got to say to you, and you're gonna listen. I've had just about enough of your complaining, your constant interfering and moaning. No one gives a toss about you and your bridge lot – a bunch of stuck-up fusspots, thinking you're better than anyone else. Not one single person in this village likes you or wants to have anything to do with you. You're nothing but a dried-up old fruit – even your husband probably can't bear the sight of you, 'cept he's too scared to say so. So why don't you do us all a favour and take your bleddy whingeing and your bleddy whining and stick 'em right up that fat arse of yorn.'

The table sat in stunned silence as Piran's words hit home. For a moment, Audrey's mouth formed into a perfect O. She tried to speak but could only manage a strangled whimper, and Helen was horrified to see that there were tears in her eyes. As if hoping that they would leap to her defence, Audrey turned helplessly to the others at the table.

Simon was first on his feet. 'Audrey, it isn't true, we're all so grateful to you for all the things you do . . .'

But Audrey stepped away from his outstretched hand. With great difficulty she found her voice. 'Well. Good evening, Reverend. Thank you for your time.'

And with that, she walked slowly and with great dignity towards her husband. Geoffrey, who'd been too far away to hear the exchange, registered that something was wrong and hurried towards her with a concerned look on his face. Audrey merely shook her head in response to his questions and made for the door, head bowed. With one last questioning glance at their table, Geoffrey followed her out.

Aghast, the three friends turned as one to Piran.

'How could you?' Helen found it hard to believe that the man she loved could be so cruel.

'You went too far there,' agreed Penny. 'Poor Audrey. I know she can be a complete pain, but she isn't a bad person and she didn't deserve that.'

Piran turned to Simon, waiting for him to add some rebuke, but he remained silent. The two men looked at each other for a moment and then Piran picked up his woollen hat and coat and walked out of the pub without another word.

'I just don't know what's wrong with him lately,' said Helen, as much to herself as anyone else. This wasn't boding at all well for Christmas.

While Penny and Helen wondered aloud what could have caused Piran to snap that way, Simon sat in silence, staring at the door that had closed behind his friend, keeping his thoughts to himself.

2

Finally giving up on the doorbell, Helen stepped back for one last look at Piran's cottage before returning to the car. She climbed into the driver's seat, rummaged in her bag for her mobile and hit the speed-dial button for what seemed the hundredth time that morning. Piran wasn't at home and had clearly turned his phone off. Once more she heard the familiar robotic voice: *It has not been possible to connect your call . . .*

She pressed the Call End button and silently cursed Piran Ambrose. He'd volunteered weeks ago to come over on Christmas Eve and help her prepare for their big feast tomorrow. It was going to be roast turkey with all the trimmings, and Piran had been the one who'd insisted that the preparations would have to be done in advance if the big day was to be a success.

Helen was making a simple starter of smoked salmon with prawn and salmon roe, but there was stuffing to make (Piran would never countenance anything so ordinary as Paxo, though Helen was a bit partial to it herself), parsnips and potatoes to parboil, giblets to be boiled and turned into stock for gravy – for which Piran had some secret recipe – pigs in blankets to prepare, not to mention their little ritual of injecting the Christmas pudding with another syringe full of brandy. They would be lucky if they didn't set the whole of Pendruggan ablaze when they lit the flame tomorrow, it was that potent.

It wasn't the end of the world that Piran hadn't shown up as arranged, but after last night's rotten business with Audrey at the pub, Helen couldn't help but feel anxious about him. She gazed up at his window and let out another sigh of frustration. Trust her to bag herself a mercurial so-and-so like Piran Ambrose! But no matter how she tried to pass it off as just Piran being moody as per usual, she couldn't help feeling that this time there was more to it.

She pushed the thought away, reminding

herself that Sean, Terri and Summer were back at Gull's Cry waiting for her. She was determined to see to it that they had the best Christmas possible, regardless of Piran and his moods. He'd just have to pull himself together, and that was that.

No sooner had she put the key in the ignition than her phone rang. She felt a thrill of pleasure when the caller ID flashed and she saw it was her daughter Chloe.

'Chloe, darling! Where are you? I miss you so much!'

'Mummy, hello, I'm fine. Everything is OK here.'

'Remind me where here is? I keep forgetting!'

'Oh, Mum, stop teasing! You know full well I'm in Madagascar. We've been exploring some of the most remote parts of Masoala National Park – you wouldn't believe how amazing it is. Tomorrow, we'll be staying somewhere there's an Internet connection, so I'll send photos.'

'Make sure there are some pictures of you too and not just the monkeys! I want to see you're all right. You're still my little girl and it's so far away, I can't help worrying. I hope you've got nice people out there taking care of you.'

'Everyone is lovely, Mum, and like me, all they want to do is help protect the environment here. We're trying to support the locals' efforts to stop logging companies from destroying any more of the rainforest.'

'Oh, darling, I know it is what you want to do and I'm so proud, but I do wish you were here with us. Summer is growing so fast.'

'I know, I Skyped Sean and Terri the other night. They reckon she looks a bit like me.'

'She does a bit, but she's got Terri's eyes.'

'How is everything else? How are you and Piran getting on?'

'Oh, you know what Piran's like.'

'Impossible?'

'That's the word!'

They both laughed. It felt so good to hear Chloe's voice.

'When are you coming home, darling? Whenever I see Mack on the beach messing about with his surfboard, he always asks after you.'

'Soon, Mum. Tell him soon.'

'I will, sweetheart,' said Helen. She could hear someone in the background yelling to Chloe to end the call, the bus would be leaving any moment. 'Bye, Chloe – love you. And don't forget to call your father!'

'I won't! Love you too, Mum. I'll Skype tomorrow,' Chloe promised and rang off.

Oh, damn, thought Helen as she started the car. *I forgot breadsticks!*

*

It seemed the whole of Trevay were busily stocking up on last-minute items, as if the shops would be closed for weeks instead of a few days. Helen darted in and out, picking up a few more crackers, some chocolate decorations that Summer could dress the tree with, more Sellotape, more wrapping paper and a big slab of smoked bacon rashers, which would do for breakfast on Christmas morning and for dressing the turkey with. As she went about her errands she scanned the crowds for a familiar face, but there was still no sign of Piran.

Heading back into Pendruggan, she passed by The Dolphin. Don, the pub's owner, was busily rolling a barrel from the back of his pickup truck towards the pub. When Helen tooted, he abandoned his barrel and waved for her to stop.

'What have you got there, Don?'

'Ah, this, this here is me special Pendruggan Christmas Ale. Comes from a secret brewery that only I knows about and I can only get me hands on one barrel a year. Folks come from far and wide to try this. We crack it open on Christmas morning and it's all gone by lunchtime.'

'Secret?' Don's wife, Dorrie, suddenly appeared in the pub doorway, wiping her hands on a tea towel. 'Nothing secret about it at all. He brews it in his shed and drinks most of it himself on the day!' They laughed good-naturedly at this and Helen laughed along with them.

'Well, I might be along to try it myself.'

'Make sure you bring that Piran Ambrose with you 'n' all. He's quite partial to a bit of this.'

'I'll try, Don – if I ever find him.'

'Find him? Well, he be down on his boat – I were out over Trevay Harbour way and I saw him. Set to be there all day from the look of 'im.'

'Oh. I see . . .' Piran used his boat the way a lot of men used their potting sheds. It served a purpose that went beyond fishing trips – he used it as a place to think. Or a place to be alone. Why had he gone out there today of all days, knowing that she was counting on his help?

'Thanks, Don. Save some of that ale for me!'

'Ah, no special treatment, I'm afraid, you'll just have to be early doors tomorrow!' he called after her as she gave another toot of the horn and drove off.

*

When she got home, Helen insisted that Sean and Terri leave Summer to her while they had some time to themselves. They needed little encouragement; within minutes they'd grabbed their coats and set off for a bracing walk along the cliffs.

'And stop by The Dolphin for a pub lunch,' she urged as she and Summer waved goodbye from the cottage door. 'There's no rush to get back. Summer and I can have an afternoon together, can't we, darling girl?'

'Gan Gan!' Summer gave her another sloppy kiss.

Helen was pleased when Summer went straight down in her travel cot. Her parenting skills – or grandparenting? – were coming back and as she gazed down at her granddaughter's angelic features, she kept her fingers crossed that Summer's teething pains wouldn't disturb her slumber.

Putting her feet up for five minutes, she called Penny and told her about Piran's disappearing act.

'Do you think he'll remember our plans for tonight?' Penny asked.

That evening, the village green was to be given over to a carol concert and the entire village would be there. A huge Christmas tree decked with hundreds of multicoloured lights had been erected on the green. When darkness fell and everyone gathered round it, the atmosphere would be magical; it was something everyone looked forward to each year. Afterwards, they were all going to head over to Trevay for a curry. It wouldn't be that late, so Sean, Terri and Summer were going to come along too. Piran adored Summer, but he hadn't been in to see her since she arrived. *Stop it*, Helen told herself, knowing that if she thought about it too much she'd get cross.

'He'll remember,' she assured Penny, 'if he knows what's good for him. I've been looking forward to it for ages, so he'd better not let me down tonight as well.'

*

The rest of the day passed without a peep from Piran. Helen had tried his phone once or twice, each time with the same result. She kept herself busy, and tried to stay jolly with Christmas music playing in the kitchen as she ticked off as many of the necessary preparations as she could. She'd got out the ice-cream maker and had enjoyed making a rich vanilla ice cream. Tomorrow, she was planning to take some of the Christmas pudding and churn it in with the ice cream with a drop or two of rum. She'd then freeze it again into a block and then later on, when their dinner had gone down a bit and they were watching telly, she would cut it into thick slabs, stick the slabs between two wafers and serve them up as a lovely decadent Christmassy take on a childhood favourite.

Despite her best efforts, there was no denying that Piran's absence had taken some of the enjoyment out of it. Helen couldn't stop herself running to the window every time she heard a vehicle, hoping to see his battered truck pulling up outside.

It was now early evening and almost time to set off for the carol singing. Terri and Sean had enjoyed their walk and then gone for a little nap upstairs while she and Summer watched *Finding Nemo* on TV. When her parents started to stir, Summer had insisted on joining them upstairs on their bed. Now Helen could hear them all getting ready, singing songs and enjoying being together. It made her smile to hear them.

This time when she ran to the window at the sound of a pickup on the lane, her heart leapt as she saw Piran climb out, leaving Jack, his faithful Jack Russell terrier, gazing out of the window.

Helen was at the door before he had even got halfway up the path. He looked tired and troubled, but at the same time she could see that streak of defiance in his eyes. His black corkscrew curls were wilder than ever after being blown about on the boat all day and Helen felt slightly annoyed at herself for finding him incredibly sexy when she ought by rights to be angry. She only hoped he had a change of clothes in the car, because he was still in his oilskins and he couldn't join them for carols and a curry dressed like that.

He remained stubbornly on the path and when Helen opened her mouth to speak, he silenced her with a raised hand.

'Before you say anything, I'm not coming tonight. I've been working on the boat all day and I'm tired.'

'But why were you working on it today of all days? You knew how much we had to do – and you haven't even come by to say hello to Summer yet.'

Far from offering an apology, he glowered at her. 'Why do I always have to fit in with you?'

'What do you mean?' said Helen, flummoxed.

'You know what I mean. These things that we "have to do" are things that you want to do – not me. I don't remember signing up for anything.'

Helen found herself at a loss. Where on earth had all this bad humour come from – they were meant to love each other, weren't they? 'But, Piran, it's Christmas . . .' was all she could come up with.

'Christmas? What do I care for Christmas?' Piran's voice was cold. 'From what I can see, Christmas is one more excuse for folks to spend obscene amounts of money on useless presents that no one wants, and send each other pointless cards that spout glib phrases like "goodwill to all men" – which no one ever means, let alone acts upon. Christmas means nothing to me and will never mean anything to me, so I don't care about dreary carols on the green, I don't care about a mediocre curry in Trevay, listening to Penny drone on endlessly about zed-list celebrities in London, I don't care about Midnight Mass. I don't care about Christmas, Helen, and I certainly don't care about—'

For a horrible moment, Helen thought he was going to say, 'I don't care about you.' But she never found out what he was going to say because they were interrupted by the sound of footsteps.

They both turned to see a troupe of little girls in brown and yellow uniforms marching down the lane and into the village. Wrapped up warmly in hats and gloves, they were ushered towards Helen's front door by the jaunty Emma Scott, Brown Owl. There weren't very many of them, but what the Pendruggan Brownies lacked in number they made up for in enthusiasm and they could often be seen around the village, trying to win their badges for map-reading skills or road safety.

'Good evening and Merry Christmas to you!' Brown Owl said cheerfully. Helen returned the smile as best she could, despite feeling bruised by Piran's outburst.

'We're doing a bit of carol singing to raise funds for the pony sanctuary before we head over to the green to join in with everyone else.'

Without waiting for a response, Brown Owl turned to the girls and gave the command: 'Right, after three. One. Two. Three . . .'

Half the girls immediately put their recorders to their lips while the others began to sing 'Good King Wenceslas'.

Helen couldn't decide if it was the discordant recorders that were the problem or the funereal quality to the singing, but either way the performance was lamentable. Still, it was all for a good cause, so she darted inside to fetch her purse. When she came back out, she was dismayed to find Piran standing in front of the group with his hands held up.

'Stop!' he shouted. 'Just stop!'

The music trailed off and the children and Brown Owl stood open-mouthed.

'What's the problem?' asked Emma.

'What's the problem?' barked Piran. 'I'll tell you what the problem is. Without a shadow of a doubt, that dirge that you and your Brownies have vomited out is a crime against nature. A dying nanny-goat would sound more melodious than this lot! What badge are they trying for this time – systematic torture?'

For a moment, there was a deathly silence. Then a small noise came from somewhere in the group and Helen, already horrified by Piran's outburst, was mortified to see that the little Brownie at the front had started to cry. One by one, the other Brownies followed suit.

Single-handed, Piran had turned the cheerful little pack of Brownies into a wailing mass of misery.

Helen's shock turned to outrage.

'Right, Piran Ambrose, this is the final straw! Over the last few weeks, you've managed to royally piss off every single one of your friends and upset practically the entire village. But this –' Here she pointed at the Brownies – 'this is a new low.'

Having said her piece, she stepped out onto the path and began to shush and comfort the little girls, while their leader stood by, dazed into stunned silence.

'Come on inside, girls. I'll make you all a hot chocolate and you can sprinkle marshmallows into it – won't that be fun?'

The idea of this yummy confection was already starting to cheer some of the girls up as she shooed them into the house.

When the last Brownie had passed through the door, Helen turned to Piran, who was standing in his oilskins, watching in silence.

'We all know you can be a moody bugger, Piran, but I've always believed that you're a good person. It looks like I might have been wrong. Maybe the message of Christmas does get lost sometimes, but turning yourself into a latterday Ebenezer Scrooge is much, much worse. I never thought I'd say this, but unless you have a major personality transplant, you're not welcome here. Not on Christmas Day. Not ever!'

She was about to head inside when she turned back for one parting shot:

'Oh, and for the record, Penny never, ever drones on about zed-list celebrities in London.'

With that, she firmly shut the door behind her.

Turning on his heel, Piran marched back to his pickup.

Christmas, he said to himself. *Bah, humbug!*

3

The lock on Carrack Cottage was inclined to be temperamental but Piran had no patience with it tonight as he rattled the key in the hole, wanting nothing more than to get inside and shut the rest of the world out.

A traditional fisherman's cottage of grey weathered Cornish stone, Carrack stood in glorious isolation at the end of a dead-end track on the outskirts of Pendruggan, not far from Shellsand Bay. There was nothing twee or touristy about the place; the only adornments on the outer walls were an old gas lamp, which had been converted to electricity, and a distressed and battered life buoy from HMS *Firebrand* that hung on a hook above the doorway. This was his inner sanctum, and he had no intention of sharing it full time with anybody. Nobody with two legs, at any rate.

Jack trotted ahead of him into the low-ceilinged room and went straight to the tatty old sofa, disturbing the two stray cats who had adopted Carrack Cottage as their home. Sprat the tabby and Bosun, who was as black as coal, jumped down from their usual spot on the cushions, leaving a trail of cat hairs behind them. Piran often suspected they didn't care who lived there as long as they got the best seats.

The cottage was filled with old furniture that had seen better days, but Piran saw no need to replace or refurbish anything. It suited him just the way it was. Evidence of his profession as an historian littered every surface. Ancient rolled-up maps of Cornwall were propped against the walls and the dusty bookshelves were crammed with tomes on everything from local history to works by Pliny. And then there was the paraphernalia relating to his other obsession: fishing. The TV stood on a lobster pot; the hallway and the pantry leading out into the small back yard were cluttered with lobster nets, fishing rods, tackle and fly lines; the cooler boxes he stored bait in were standing ready by the back door, alongside his waders.

Still in the blackest of moods, he took off his oilskins and hung them up, then began rummaging through the cupboards for a tin of pilchards to feed the cats. Something brushed by his heel and he turned to see Jack, soulful brown eyes following his every move. He reached into the cupboard for a second tin of pilchards. They'd have to do for Jack as well.

The smell of the pilchards made Piran's stomach rumble, so when he'd finished dishing out the gooey mixture of fish and tomato sauce, he went to his ancient fridge in search of sustenance. The tiny freezer compartment was permanently frozen up and he stared dispiritedly at the fridge's contents: half a packet of unsalted butter, half a lemon and a bit of slightly tired cheddar. The bread bin was empty. Piran cursed. Of course there wasn't anything to eat. He was supposed to be staying at Helen's place for the next few days, so there'd been no reason to stock up with supplies. The phrase 'biting off your nose to spite your face' popped into his head. Dismissing it, he set his lips into a thin line and went back to the cupboard for a third tin. If pilchards were good enough for the dog and cats, then they were good enough for him.

'Nothing wrong with pilchards, boy,' he said out loud. 'Would've fallen on them like a starving man when I was a lad.'

He took the plate of pilchards, to which he'd added the last of the cheese, into the small living room, and turned on the TV. Settling himself in front of it, he took a mouthful of pilchards and decided that things definitely weren't what they used to be. Rubbing at his eyes as tiredness crept in, he decided there was nothing for it but to make do with the cheese alone.

He flicked through the channels: *Morecambe and Wise Christmas Special* – click; *Eight Out of Ten Cats Does Countdown* – click; some idiot extolling the virtues of lawnmowers on the Shopping Channel. 'In December?' *Click*.

The next channel he clicked on was a film, so old it was in black and white. Piran thought he recognised the actor, though he couldn't think of his name, but the story was instantly identifiable: *A Christmas Carol*. What was it Helen had said about him being a latterday Scrooge? Piran knitted his brow but continued watching.

On the screen, Scrooge woke to find he had

a visitor: the ghost of his former partner, Jacob Marley. Dragging heavy chains behind him, Marley was telling Scrooge *these are the chains I forged in life . . . you do not know the weight and length of strong chain you bear yourself . . . it was as full and as long as this seven Christmases ago and you have laboured on it since . . .*

Christmas Eve – it was inevitable they'd be broadcasting this old stalwart. Nothing coincidental about it, Piran told himself, watching Scrooge cringe and writhe as Marley's spirit clanked his chains and listed his torments:

I am doomed to wander without rest or peace . . . incessant torture and remorse . . .

Overwhelmed with a deep tiredness, Piran felt his eyelids begin to droop.

Hear me, my time is nearly gone . . . I come tonight to warn you that you have yet a chance of escaping my fate . . .

Despite the pull of sleep, the voice continued, drifting through his drowsy consciousness:

You will be visited by three spirits . . . without their help you cannot hope to shun the path I tread . . . hope to see me no more . . .

*

Piran woke with a start, disturbed by a loud knocking on his front door. Disoriented and with sleep still clinging to him, it took a moment to realise that the cottage was in total darkness. Scrooge and Marley were gone, the TV screen was blank. The lamps were out and the only light came from the waning moon-light that filtered in through the front windows.

Another rap on the front door. In the dark-ness, Piran picked his way over the plate that had held his pilchards, polished off long ago by the cats, and tried to find his way through the dark. Flicking the light switches on the walls elicited no response, either in the living room or in the kitchen, and Piran wondered if the fuses had blown.

He was almost at the front door when he tripped over one of the fishing rods that was leaning up against the wall. Falling forward, he banged his head painfully on the coat stand.

'Bollocks!'

As he untangled himself, someone banged on the front door again.

'All right, keep your bleddy 'air on, will you!' he muttered, fumbling with the lock and wrenching the door open.

Only to find that there was absolutely no one there.

What the hell was going on? No lights or power and now a phantom at the doorway? Piran wasn't sure where he had got the word phantom from but he suddenly felt unsettled. There were no such things as ghosts, so someone must have been knocking at his door – but where were they now?

He took a step out onto the path and peered into the gloom. He could see no one, and when he looked up the road towards the village he realised that was in darkness too. His position on the edge of Pendruggan meant that he could usually see the distant lights of shops and houses – but tonight there was nothing. It gave the night an eerie feel. Almost as if the village had vanished and he was the only one left . . .

'Things look different in the dark, don't they?'

'*Argh*!' Piran nearly jumped out of his skin when the voice came out of the pitch-black.

Then the voice again, and light from a torch illuminating a familiar face. 'It's only me.'

'Bleddy hell, Simon! Where the 'ell 'ave you come from?'

'Sorry, Piran. You're not normally so jumpy.' Piran wasn't sure what he had expected, but it was a relief to see Simon's cheery face. 'I was knocking for ages. I knew you must be in because I could hear Jack scrabbling at the door, so I nipped round to see if the back door was open. But it wasn't.'

Piran rubbed his hands across his eyes as if to rub away the last vestiges of sleep that still seemed to linger.

'What the hell is going on?'

'Power cut. The whole village is out.'

'Shit!'

'Indeed. Are you planning on inviting me in? It's freezing out here.'

Piran grunted his assent and the two of them, using Simon's torch as a guide, led the way inside.

'Gimme that torch and wait here.' Simon did as he was told and Piran headed off to the pantry. After much rummaging and rustling, he reappeared, carrying a handful of fat candles. Handing the torch back to Simon, Piran proceeded to stick them into candle holders. Before long, the room was lit by gentle candlelight.

'Save your batteries,' he said.

Simon switched off his torch and sat down. Piran checked the clock; almost eleven. He'd been asleep for hours.

'What are you doing abroad?' he asked.

'Well, I'm worried that some of the villagers won't be able to get to Midnight Mass because they don't all have cars and the roads are too dark. I've got my car and I'm going to have a recce and see if anyone needs a lift.'

'So what brings you here?'

'Ah, well . . .' Simon blinked back at him, abashed. 'I was wondering if you're all right?'

'Why wouldn't I be all right?' Piran demanded.

Simon hesitated, trying to find the right words. 'Piran, I know that you hate talking about . . . well, things . . . emotions and the like. All the same, we have known each other for a long time and I can tell when something is up.'

Piran turned away, avoiding Simon's eyes. 'There's nothing up.'

Undaunted, Simon continued: 'The last few weeks, you've been really . . . pent up, and it's obvious there's more to it than the usual trade-mark Mr Mean persona that you like to hide behind. I can see right through you, Piran. Is this something to do with Jenna?'

At the mention of her name, Piran leapt to his feet and rounded on Simon. 'Why don't you just mind your own business? Maybe the rest of Pendruggan like to spill their guts out in the confessional, but I can do without your cod philosophy, Vicar.'

Though his words stung, Simon persisted: 'Firstly, for the record, I'm a Church of England vicar not a Catholic priest, and we don't have a confession box in Pendruggan. Secondly, and more importantly, I'm your friend and I can tell you're bottling something up.'

Piran glared at Simon for a moment. Then he sighed and sat down.

'I don't know what it is. I can't seem to shake it off. Feel like I'm fed up with everything. Christmas only seems to have made it worse.'

'A problem shared?'

'I dunno, Simon. Don't feel I want to share right now. Perhaps this is the way that I'm destined to be from now on.'

'Rubbish! You weren't always like this.'

'Wasn't I?'

'Certainly not! You used to be quite carefree

when you were younger. Remember that year when we did the Pendruggan Christmas swim?'

'We've done it more than once.'

'Yes, but no other year was like this one . . .'

4

1984

*P*iran's face broke into a smile as he saw Simon walking down the sloping slip road that lead towards Pendruggan's harbour. He'd been sitting, waiting, huddled up in his parka in the wintery sunshine, having called Simon last night to let him know that he was back in Pendruggan.

After a warm embrace and the customary ruffling of each other's hair, Simon stood back and took a good look at his friend. Piran's skin was the colour of golden caramel, his black curls were thicker and more unruly than he remembered and his piercing blue eyes were glimmering roguishly. A long summer spent island-hopping in Greece had served only to accentuate Piran's piratical appearance and the acquisition of a small hooped gold earring finished off the look perfectly. If Simon hadn't already known that Piran didn't give a toss about his looks, he might have suspected he'd done it on purpose, but there wasn't a vain bone in Piran's body.

'Where did the earring come from?'

Piran grinned sheepishly. 'Can't quite remember. A few too many ouzos one night in Mykonos. More trouble to take it out, I reckon.'

'How was Greece? Feels like you've been away for ever.'

'Only five months. But Greece in winter loses a bit of its shine. The tourists all bugger off and there's no bar work to speak of. I was ready to come home, anyhow. What about you, Canter? You're as milky white as you were at Easter. What have you been up to?'

'Come on. I'll tell you over a pint at The Dolphin.'

At the bar, Piran ordered them both two pints of Best and a couple of packets of Smiths crisps, while Simon lined up a few tracks on the jukebox. Piran was more of a Led Zeppelin or Pink Floyd man, but Simon couldn't resist a bit of pop and this was a vintage year. Which ones to choose? He settled on 'Two Tribes' by Frankie Goes to

Hollywood, 'Wild Boys' by Duran Duran and 'Wake Me Up' by Wham! – but that was chiefly to annoy Piran.

At the bar, Piran was accosted by the young barman, Don.

'Oi, Ambrose, where you been lately? Not round these parts, judging by that suntan. My sister, Jenna, been wondering on that only the other day.'

Piran hoped that his tan covered the flush that he felt in his cheeks at the mention of Jenna's name.

'I've been travelling, Don. How is Jenna?'

'Well, you're not the only one been getting themselves about. Jenna finished her teacher training and now she's been offered a job in London, she 'as.'

Don's older sister was the same age as Piran and he'd been attracted to her ever since he could remember. They'd been more than friends at one time, but somehow, with his years away at Cambridge and her teacher training, they'd barely seen each other since leaving school. 'That's great news, Don. Give her my best.'

Don's eyes twinkled mischievously. 'She'll be here in a minute – she's been helping out, doing a few shifts – so you can tell 'er yourself.'

The thought that she might be along any minute gave Piran a thrill of excitement that he did his best to conceal as he was joined at the bar by Simon. A moment later, the high-energy bass of 'Two Tribes' and Holly Johnson's nasal Liverpudlian tones burst from the jukebox.

'Oi, keep it down. This ain't the Hammersmith Palais, yer know!'

Piran and Simon looked over their shoulders to see Queenie, the local postmistress and proprietor of the village shop, sitting at a corner table with a port and lemon in front of her. 'Welcome back, Piran! Come and have one of me pasties as an homecoming present – you can 'ave it on the 'ouse!'

'Thanks, Queenie, I'll be over in the morning.'

'Here, Don,' Piran handed over a one-pound note. 'Get Queenie another.'

'Anyway, Ambrose . . .' Don picked out a bottle of Cockburn's and poured a couple of fingers' worth into a glass '. . . reckon you've been keeping a low profile these last few years 'cos you're frightened of getting beaten again on the swim.'

'That what you reckon, is it, Don?'

The Christmas Day swim was an annual institution in the village, drawing people from miles around. Most came to spectate, but many took part. For the majority it was nothing more than the precursor to their first brandy of the day, and a bit of a laugh – no wetsuits were allowed and some of the more exhibitionist participants ventured forth in the nude, usually to cheers of encouragement from the rowdy crowd. There were, however, a hardcore of experienced swimmers who raced out to the buoy and back again, determined to claim the honour of pulling and downing the first pint of the celebrated, home-brewed Christmas Day Ale from the special Pendruggan tankard at The Dolphin. Both members of this elite, Piran and Don had a rivalry that went back years.

'Maybe I've been doing you a favour by not showing up,' laughed Piran. 'Not sure how happy you'd be to have a bit of decent competition.' He eyed Don's beer belly. 'Looks like you've been enjoying the beers and pies too much, mate.'

Don frowned. 'Oi, that's not fat! Hundred per cent Cornish muscle, that is!'

Simon and Piran spluttered and guffawed over their pints.

'You might laugh, Ambrose, but ain't many in Pendruggan faster than me in the water, you included.'

'That's fighting talk that is, Don.' Piran said this with a telltale twinkle in his eyes that revealed there was nothing he liked more than a challenge.

'You're out of the running, mate. Leave it to the younger ones like me,' Don jeered. He pointed to the barrel conspicuously placed at the bottom of the bar. It was covered in tinsel and lights and a handwritten note stuck to it proclaimed: Winner takes all!

'That barrel ain't got my name on it yet, Ambrose, but come Christmas morning it'll be me supping that lovely golden liquid.'

Piran picked up their pints. 'Thanks, Don – here, have something for yourself . . .' He placed another one-pound note on the counter. 'Reckon you'll need it to buy your own pints on Christmas Day.'

Don gave him a two-fingered salute but pocketed the pound all the same.

They took their seats and Simon began filling him in on all the local news, but Piran was impatient to hear what Simon himself had been up to.

'Well, actually, there is something I've been meaning to tell you.'

'What is it?'

'Well . . .' Simon played nervously with a beer mat.

'Come on, man, spit it out!'

'Remember I told you that I was going to stay on at Oxford and do a Masters?'

'In Theology? Yes, why? Have you changed your mind?'

'Yes. No. Well, not exactly . . .'

'Oh, for heaven's sake!' spluttered Piran, infuriated. 'Tell you what, why don't I finish it for you. You've decided to do your Masters and after that you're going to become a priest.'

Simon gawped at his friend in astonishment. 'How did you know?'

Piran laughed and put his arm around Simon's shoulder. 'I've always known, mate. Even if you didn't. All those drunken late-night chats about the nature of God and the universe? Most men our age would've been thinking about nookie, but not you.'

Simon's face betrayed uncertainty. 'Do you think I'm making the right decision? You don't mind?'

'Mind!' Piran gave Simon a giant bearhug. 'I can't think of a better man for the job. You'll *make a great vicar! And if I ever find the right girl, I want you to marry us – you can also christen any unlucky offspring I might have. And when the music's over, I want you to turn out the lights and give me the last rites. Mind? I'm relying on you!'*

As if on cue, the door to the pub opened and in walked Jenna. She didn't see the two men immediately and made straight for the bar. Piran watched her nervously and rubbed his hands on his 501s.

'Go on – say hello,' Simon urged.

Jenna was even lovelier than he remembered. She removed her red beret, purple velvet jacket and crocheted bag, then hung them all on a hook behind the bar. Her hair was the colour of wet sand and it took a moment before her clear blue eyes spotted him. When they did, she clapped her hands and a smile lit up her face.

'Piran!' She ran out from behind the bar and rushed over to their table. He stood and she threw her arms around him warmly. 'You're a sight for sore eyes, Piran Ambrose!'

Jenna barely worked her shift that night, much to her grumbling brother's annoyance. When Simon headed home a few pints later, Piran and

Jenna were still ensconced at the bar, heads close together; talking and laughing and in no hurry to go home themselves.

*

Piran and Simon jumped up and down and rubbed their bare arms to try to keep themselves warm. It was Christmas morning and it seemed the whole of Trevay and Pendruggan had come along to the Christmas Day swim on Shellsand Bay, though the hardy souls who were willing to brace the Atlantic waters were vastly outnumbered by spectators. The ban on wetsuits had separated the wheat from the chaff; although the distance between the shore and the buoy wasn't far, the water was only a few degrees above freezing at this time of year and it could be gruelling.

Throngs of people lined the shore, a barbecue had been set up and someone was serving bacon sandwiches while flasks of firewater were passed round; the mood was jovial and good-humoured; a gang of teenagers wore Santa hats and were singing a raucous rendition of 'Rudolf the Red-Nosed Reindeer', but in their version it was another part of Rudolf's anatomy that was going down in history. Conditions were good; despite the cold, it was a clear morning with just a hint of the morning mist in the air.

Don, already stripped down to his Speedos, came over and slapped them both on the back.

'It's colder than a witch's tit out here!' He laughed. 'Ready for a good pasting, boys?'

Unlike Simon, who was waiting until the last minute to strip off, Piran was primed for action, his goggles sitting on his head in readiness.

'Don't be writing cheques your butt can't cash, boy.' He poked Don's stomach good-naturedly.

Jenna joined them and put an arm around each of their shoulders as they towered over her petite and slender frame.

'Ah, my two favourite Pendruggan boys!'

'Who are you putting your money on, Jenna?' Simon asked through chattering teeth.

'I couldn't possibly comment,' she replied enigmatically, refusing to be drawn, but she eyed Piran's tanned and taut six-pack admiringly. Simon saw a look pass between them and decided that things had definitely moved on since their night in The Dolphin.

At that moment, the sound of a loud bell rang

out across the water. The adjudicator was the landlord of the pub, Peter. He was holding a large church bell, the same one he used to call time, and was exhorting the gathered participants to take their places.

The men and women who were taking part lined up and, when Peter fired the starting pistol, they all plunged into the sea. The coldness of the water took Piran's breath away. The last time he'd swum in the sea it had been in the warm waters of a crystal-clear Greek lagoon, but this was something else entirely. He forced himself to focus on keeping his limbs moving and progressed quickly through the water. He sensed that Don was a little way behind him – they were both strong swimmers but Piran's active summer seemed to be giving him the edge today and his pace quickened as the adrenalin coursed through his body, energising his muscles. He approached the buoy and risked a glance around. To his surprise and elation he was well out in front. Don seemed to have dropped back.

Having reached the buoy, Piran turned over in the water and kicked off for the return leg. He passed other swimmers on the way, all intent on reaching the buoy, but Don wasn't among *them. Slightly ahead, between him and the shoreline, he could see a figure in the water. His immediate instinct was to adjust his course in order to avoid a head-on collision, but then he realised that the person in the water was Don. How had he managed to get this far ahead? Stung into action, Piran picked up speed in the hope of overtaking him. But as he passed, some sixth sense made him slow and turn his head. It was then he realised that Don was in trouble, desperately treading water, his face ashen.*

Within moments, Piran was by Don's side. 'What's wrong, buddy?'

It was all Don could do to gasp out two words: 'Can't breathe.'

Piran looked towards the beach, trying to make out the lifeguard, but it was difficult to see from this distance. It was going to be down to him to get Don back to shore – and fast.

'Right, here's what we're going to do,' he commanded. 'Put your arms around my neck from the back and I'll swim us to shore, like they do in the movies.'

Too weak to argue, Don gripped Piran as best he could and they progressed slowly through the water, Don's rasping and ragged breath sounding in Piran's ear. Piran was beginning to tire when Simon came alongside to help. Before long they were nearing the shore, where the lifeguard paddled out in his canoe to meet them.

*

Don puffed hard on his inhaler. He was sitting on a camping chair, wrapped in towels and blankets, flanked by Jenna, Simon and Piran. The colour was back in his cheeks and his asthma attack was now well under control.

'Felt a bit wheezy this morning, but didn't wanna miss it.'

'You dafty. You could have drowned out there,' Jenna chided, but she was too relieved that her brother was going to be OK to be angry with him.

'Just glad I brought this with me. Don't have much call for it these days. Thought I'd grown out of the old asthma.' He took another puff. 'But it's thanks to Blackbeard here that it weren't worse. Good of you to help out, mate.' He looked gratefully towards Piran, as did Jenna, whose eyes shone with admiration and gratitude.

'Anyone would've done the same,' he replied,

scoffing at the suggestion his actions had been in any way heroic.

'Not sure they would have if they was in the lead and looking forward to that Christmas Ale.'

'Who won in the end?'

'Not sure . . . come on, let's get down to The Dolphin and find out – we can't have them drinking all that ale without us now, can we?'

With that, the four friends headed off to the pub, singing 'Rudolph the Red-Knobbed Reindeer' . . .

*

'Jenna never did take that job in London,' said Piran, the long shadows cast by the candlelight flickering against the living-room walls.

'She went to work at Trevay Juniors, didn't she?' said Simon.

'She loved it there. Really got a kick out of seeing the kids thrive.'

'I remember how good she was with children. Always giving of her time. Didn't she volunteer at the hospital over the holidays?'

'That's right – and she usually managed to rope in a few others as well. She was nothing if not persuasive.'

'Tell me about it!' agreed Simon. 'On one of my first Christmas visits home after joining the seminary, she had me dressed up as Father Christmas, giving out donated presents to the kids in the children's ward at Trevay's old cottage hospital.'

Piran remembered it well. 'Didn't one young boy accuse you of being a fake because everyone knew Santa didn't have ginger hair and glasses?'

They both laughed at the memory.

'Then there was the other Christmas.' Piran's face clouded over again.

'The one where she . . .' Simon hesitated.

'Died. That's the word you're looking for, Simon. Yes, the Christmas where that bloody maniac . . . The hit and run . . . Police never got him.'

They both fell silent, thinking back to that terrible time. It was Simon who broke the silence.

'Bad things happen all year round, Piran. Good things, too. Christmas is just a reminder of how we should be three hundred and sixty-five days of the year. It isn't always possible and we're only human, but we can strive. What was it that Scrooge said, after his moment of epiphany?'

Piran's eyes narrowed – what was this obsession everyone had with Scrooge?

'*I will honour Christmas in my heart, and try to keep it all the year.*'

'You're too idealistic.' Piran shook his head dismissively. 'Folk only care for themselves.'

'I don't agree with you, my friend. Look around and you'll see. There is hope and love everywhere.' He stood. 'Anyway, I'd better get going. Some of the villagers will be anxious in this blackout and might need help. I suggest you might do the same yourself.'

Piran followed Simon out to the door.

'Goodwill to all men is usually found at the bottom of a glass of mulled wine and disappears along with the hangover.'

'You're so cynical these days.' Simon turned to face Piran. 'I remember something that Jenna said to me once: "A man who doesn't keep Christmas in his heart will never find it under a tree."'

He pulled on his gloves and hat. 'Goodnight, Piran, and a Merry Christmas to you.'

Then he was gone.

5

Piran didn't care what Simon said, he was too naive and trusting to know much about human nature. He wasn't worldly wise. But his words had pricked at Piran's conscience – the vicar was good at that – and anyway, he was wide awake now and might as well take a walk out and see what was happening.

Taking a torch from the ledge over the front door, he headed out towards the back yard. Opening the door to the shed, he shone his torch in, knowing that somewhere in the piles of boxes was a heavy-duty rechargeable lamp that would be more useful than the small Maglite one. Piran's shed was not a shed like most men's; it served as a workshop, with a long workbench down one wall and a dusty and cracked window overlooking the fields behind. It was packed with fishing paraphernalia, as well as several carpentry projects in various stages of development. His grandfather had been a shipwright and carpentry seemed to run in their blood. One of those projects was a doll's house that he had been making for Summer. Recently, he'd lost heart in the project and had struggled to finish it. He comforted himself with the thought that she was too young for it yet, anyway. Turning away from the abandoned project, he began rummaging through the boxes, which held everything from spanners to old copies of *Sporting Life*.

'Where is the damned thing?' he cursed as he pulled another dusty box down from the shelf.

Some of these boxes had been here for decades. *What was in this one?* He placed it on the work counter.

He shook it – nothing breakable – and then peeled away the yellowed and no-longer-sticky Sellotape that had been used to seal the box. His heart gave a jolt as he saw the contents. A hand-carved and painted Nativity set. One by one, he took out the figures: a shepherd, a donkey, one of the three kings, Mary and Joseph . . . Finally, rummaging around in the bottom, he found the manger containing Baby Jesus. Unlike the others, this remained unpainted and unfinished. Piran remembered making these. He had lovingly created every piece and now here they were – forgotten and useless. When was the last time he had made something like this – made it for the joy of simply doing it and because he could?

He sighed and placed the figures back in the box.

Eventually, he found the missing lamp and headed out into the night.

*

Piran had always thought that the light was different in Cornwall and tonight it seemed especially so. This Christmas Eve, the night was clear and the stars lit up the sky like a luminous carpet. The crescent moon was low in the sky and the dew on the grass shimmered like diamond dust on the fields.

He wasn't sure where he was going exactly but headed in the general direction of the village. There was something about the surrounding darkness that accentuated the sounds around him. Not far from the headland, he thought he could still hear the waves crashing on the shore. This part of Cornwall felt defined by the sea. He imagined this was how Pendruggan would have been before the adoption of electricity, with seafarers totally dependent on the lighthouse to keep them clear of the treacherous coast. Cornish folk had held onto the old ways for longer than many, and he remembered that even when he was a boy, some of villagers still made do with gas and candlelight, and horses and carts continued to be a fixture of village life.

Gradually, he left the headland behind and the comforting sound of the sea, and a silence seemed to fall around him as he neared the collection of houses that made up the village. It was almost as if the land was holding its breath for something. Piran wasn't easily spooked but he felt unnerved – was he being watched?

He heard something crackle behind him, as if someone or something had trodden on a twig. An owl cried out in the distance and the hedgerows rustled.

Watched? Or followed? He shone his lamp into the fields.

'Who's there?' His voice sounded strange to his own ears as it echoed in the silence.

Nothing. He continued on his way, shining the torch again.

There it was again, another crackle to his right.

He swung round, thrusting his torch over the dry stone wall that separated him from the field.

To his utter horror, an unearthly, grotesque face loomed out of the darkness at him. Its eyes were two black pools of darkness and its mouth was a red gash containing sharp yellow teeth.

'*Dear God!*' he cried out.

'Keep yer 'air on! It's only me!'

It took Piran a moment to realise that he recognised that voice and, when he did, he immediately felt like a complete fool. It was Queenie, of course, the octogenarian proprietor of the village shop. Her bright-red lipstick and NHS dentures had taken on a rather sinister aspect in the glaring light of his lamp. She peered out at him from underneath a bobble hat that resembled a tea cosy. There was no getting away from it, though – her eyes really did look like two black pools of darkness.

'What on earth are you doing out in the dark?' he asked her.

'Sorry, Piran, did I give you a fright?' She gave him one of her trademark cackles. 'I was trying to find Monty – she's gone missing. Ain't seen 'er, 'ave yer?'

'Who the hell is Monty?'

'She's a stray kitten that seems to 'ave adopted me. I called her Monty when I thought she was a boy, only she ain't. Vlad the Impaler would have been a better name. Always out on the hunt, she is, but she's as black as the night and now we got no lights I'm worried she'll get lost and not be able to find her way back.'

Piran glanced doubtfully at Queenie's birdlike legs.

'Queenie, cats can normally look after themselves, even kittens. Little old ladies wandering around in the dark don't always fare so well.'

'Oi, less of the old.'

'Come on – give me your arm. I'll walk you home.'

They headed back up to the village, Queenie all the while calling out to Monty. Piran could see in the lamplight that, despite being in darkness, the village was a hive of activity. Neighbours were darting into each other's houses, some of them carrying candles and torches, others laden with Thermos flasks filled with hot drinks.

Shortly, they were at the village store and Queenie opened the side door and let them in. It was rarely locked.

'Come in and have a snifter, why don't ya?'

'No, thanks, Queenie. I'd better be off.'

'Why, where you going? Don't be such a bloody misery guts.' She grabbed his arm and dragged him through to the back lounge, where Piran was surprised to see Colonel Stick and Simple Tony, plus a couple of old lags, Bert and Sid, that he recognised from the pub. There seemed to be a party of sorts going on in the candlelight and Queenie was thrilled when she saw Monty sitting in Tony's lap. The kitten was licking her paws and seemed very pleased with herself.

Queenie's back parlour was jam-packed with comfy old furniture and on every wall and surface were photographs of Queenie and her late husband, Ted. Piran couldn't remember ever coming in the back before; there was a cosy clutter to the place that brought to mind a gypsy caravan filled with trinkets, keepsakes, crocheted cushions and huge glass ashtrays. A warm and lively orange fire burned in the grate.

'She got a rat!' Simple Tony dangled the rat for Queenie to see.

Despite the un-PC nickname, Tony was loved by the villagers, particularly Queenie. When his mother had died, the thought of the poor lad fending for himself had bothered Queenie so much that she'd arranged for him to take up residence in a shepherd's hut, where she could keep an eye on him.

'Fer Gawd's sake, get rid of it!' Queenie cried, shooing Tony outside, then proceeded to make Piran a drink.

She thrust a Babycham cocktail glass into his hand, which was filled with a purple liquid. Piran took a sip and had to fight down his gag reflex.

'Nothing like a cherry brandy and Coke to give you that Christmassy feeling!' she cackled. 'Cheer up, Piran! Anyone would think you'd found a quid and lost a fiver!'

The others all joined in the laughter and

Piran felt his mood lift a little. Maybe it was the cherry brandy.

Colonel Stick stood and went over to look out of the window.

'People have been so kind. We've had everyone knocking at the door to make sure we're all right.'

'Yeah,' agreed Queenie, pouring herself a generous drink. 'Polly's going to bring us up to church just before midnight. It's good to know people care.'

Having made sure everyone else was comfortable, Queenie sat down. Minutes later, Tony joined them, having disposed of Monty's conquest and opened another can of Fanta for himself.

'When you're my age, you're quite used to this sort of thing, you know,' Queenie said. 'I remember once, when I was very young, growing up in London, we got caught in an air raid. This would have been Christmas 1940 – that winter saw some of the worse bombing in the Blitz. We came from the East End, but my mum and dad loved Christmas and they took us up to Oxford Street to see the window displays. It was exciting being there. Even though the city was on its knees, it never seemed to stop people going about their daily business. I don't think I'll ever forget the windows in Selfridges – I'd been looking forward to seeing them for ages, the store was famous for its window displays even in those days – but the place had been bombed a few months before and the windows were all bricked up. I started crying and my dad made it up to me by taking me into the big Woollies and buying me a liquorice stick and a toy rabbit. Then we had our tea at the Lyons Corner House. That jam scone was the loveliest thing I've ever eaten. No scone 'as been as good before or since.'

Queenie took another sip of her drink, enjoying the memory.

'It was getting dark when we came out and the Luftwaffe decided they'd start early that night. The sirens went off and we had to get down below as quickly as possible. Oxford Circus station was the closest and we had to hole up down there for what seemed like hours. The smell of all those bodies could be a bit much, but there was never any argy-bargy or trouble – we was all in the same boat, you see.

We sat around, singing songs, and Mum had wrapped up a bit of fruit cake in a hankie and we lasted on that and a bottle of squash between us. It was one of the happiest memories I've got of them – we all sang "Knees Up, Mother Brown" and "Roll Out the Barrel" . . .'

At this remembrance, she broke into 'On Mother Kelly's Doorstep' and the others in the room all joined in. Even Piran and Tony, who didn't know the words, couldn't resist humming along.

Queenie continued: 'Not long after that I was evacuated to Pendruggan. My mum couldn't bear the thought of being separated from me but London was just too dangerous by then.' She paused and took another gulp of her drink. 'It wasn't long after I came 'ere that I got the news they'd been killed when an incendiary fell on the house.'

Tears shone in her eyes. 'Bloody Jerries. Our street in Bethnal Green might have been a slum, but we called it home. I don't remember much before Cornwall, but I'll always remember that day out in London.'

She took a hanky from the cuff of her seventies nylon shirt and dabbed at her eyes with it.

'Thank God for the people around here. Good farming folk I was with who loved me like their own. I never went home again. Grew up 'ere and married my Ted.'

Queenie gazed at the photograph of Ted on the mantel, still sporting a short back and sides despite clearly being of pensionable age. 'I've been a widow for over fifteen years now . . .'

The little group struck up another song, 'Run Rabbit Run', and Queenie joined in.

The Colonel explained to Piran that they had been listening to old LPs on Queenie's ancient Dansette, but the power cut had put paid to that. The Colonel was wearing his customary blazer and MCC tie and his walking stick rested next to him on the arm of his chair.

'Bert and Sid are widowers, Tony has no family to care for him, but together with myself and Queenie, we make up a little family and we look after each other.'

He pulled out his wallet and took a photo from it, which he proudly showed to Piran. It was of a very young but instantly recognisable Colonel and he was with his regiment. They were all in their dress uniform, handsome and vital, seemingly with no inkling of what lay ahead.

'Many of us ended up in a POW camp in Korea. I remember one particularly dreadful Christmas when typhus had taken hold; many of my men were sick and some were dying. The conditions were dreadful, the heat and the insanitary conditions were impossible to describe. But we endured and we made the best of what we had. We put on shows, poking fun at the officers and of our captors and we even did a panto. One of our men, Pinky, cobbled together a little newspaper full of funny made-up stories about what was happening at home. I still have no idea how he did it – it was nothing short of a miracle.'

The Colonel stared into the distance, and it seemed to Piran as if he was gazing directly into the past – seeing Pinky and all his old comrades in his mind's eye.

'Pinky never made it back to Blighty.' He put the photograph back in his wallet. 'It was the camaraderie, the kindness and the compassion that we showed to each other that kept us all going. Many of my dear comrades suffered the same fate as Pinky, but for those that did make it home, it isn't the atrocities and the degradations of war that we remember now, rather the comradeship and friendship of our fellow men.'

Piran realised he had finished his cherry brandy. Perhaps it was the alcohol that was pricking his eyes, making them feel a little teary, or perhaps it was because he felt humbled in the presence of this small group. Despite the privations and hardships they had endured, they pulled together. They made each other's lives better by the simple act of just being there for one another. They made it seem so easy.

'Right!' Queenie drained her glass and stood up. 'Now, you'll 'ave to excuse my manners but Polly will be here shortly and I'd better get me face on. Come on, fellas – look lively!'

Piran said his goodnights to everyone and they all wished him a cheery and heartfelt Merry Christmas.

'You see,' Queenie said as she escorted him to the back door, 'all we have in this life is each other. Living through the war showed me that we're all just people. Christmas might bring us all together, but goodwill to all men is more than a phrase that you trot out once a year.' She planted a whiskery kiss on his cheek. 'You gotta keep Christmas going all year round.'

6

After the warm and cosy fug of Queenie's living room, the blast of cold air was a shock to the system. Piran pulled his jacket closer around him. Where to now? He felt strangely rootless and the thought of going back to his cold and dark cottage and being on his own again wasn't something he wanted to contemplate.

For the first time in he couldn't remember how long, he was actually craving human company. He checked his watch by the lamp-light. It was close to midnight. Without being able to explain why, he felt himself being pulled towards the spire of the church. In spite of the darkness of the night, there seemed to be a light emanating from it. As he approached, he could see that the churchyard and the path up to the large open doors were lined with dozens of little tealights and candles inside jam jars, vases and anything that could accommodate a candle without being blown out. As villagers entered the church grounds, they all added their own candles to the carpet of light – a frost was well in evidence by now and the lights lent the damp air an almost dreamlike quality.

The light from the church clock still appeared to be working and Piran thought it probably had its own power source. He could see from the dial that it was a few moments before midnight.

People were still arriving at the church, which was also full of candlelight, and he saw faces he knew and voices he recognised passing through the church door to take their seats. Even though he knew practically every single person in the church, he was anxious not to be seen, so he ducked behind one of the ancient oak trees that lined the path as the final stragglers, including Queenie and her entourage, took their seats.

The clock struck twelve. The sonorous tones of the old bell rang out across the village and the organist struck up the opening bars of the hymn 'Hark the Herald Angels Sing'. The voices of the congregation drifted out into the night and Piran found himself being pulled to the entrance, the carol acting like a siren call to his soul.

From the doorway, he saw the backs of the congregation. In the crowd, he was able to pick out Helen, Sean and Terri. Little Summer was asleep on her daddy's shoulder, her face a perfect heart shape, and Helen was gazing adoringly on her granddaughter while singing lustily, her face glowing in the candlelight. For a moment, she turned her head and looked to the back of the church, as if she was searching for someone. In his heart, Piran knew that it was he that she was hoping to see – he held his breath, hoping he wouldn't be spotted, but he was well hidden in the shadows and Helen turned away, quickly brushing away the traces of disappointment before her family noticed.

Piran felt a sudden burst of love in his heart for them all. Why wasn't he there with them? Why couldn't he simply walk right in now and take his seat next to her? What was stopping him?

With a sinking heart he realised that he knew

the answer – he didn't belong. Love, family and contentment weren't for the likes of him. That was for other folks. All of that had gone wrong for him before and it would go wrong again – he was a fool if he thought things could ever be different.

Resigned, he turned for home. But as he made to leave the churchyard, something caught his eye. Standing in front of one of the graves was a man. He held a storm light aloft and appeared to be reading the words on the headstone.

The man turned and looked directly at Piran, then held up a hand to him as if in greeting. *Who was it?* Piran slowly walked towards him and, as he approached, the other man held his gaze, never wavering or blinking.

As he neared, Piran felt a shot of recognition – he knew this man, didn't he? There was something about him that was so familiar, if he could only put his finger on it. The man was old, perhaps in his seventies or eighties, but it was hard to tell. His face was strong, and though it was heavily lined and weathered, his piercing blue eyes watched Piran intently. The man's curly hair was grey, but it would once have been the same colour as the few wisps of deep black that lingered on his temples and eyebrows.

Though he gave no greeting, the man continued to regard Piran keenly, as if he was sizing him up. Then he turned his eyes away from Piran and back to the inscription carved into the stone. He lifted his arm slowly and deliberately and pointed to the name. Piran followed the man's gaze and drew a sharp intake of breath when he saw the name inscribed there:

Perran Ambrose.

Piran knew that this spelling was a variation on his own name. The words below said:

Born 1843. Died 1911.

There was nothing else, no wife interred with him and no dedication or words of committal.

The old man's voice when he spoke was surprisingly strong. The accent was unmistakeably Cornish and by its inflection, Piran thought he sounded like a local.

'You know the name?' He directed the

question at Piran, but kept his eyes focused on the headstone.

'Of course I know the name.' How could he not?

'Then you know the name of Ambrose goes back generations here in Pendruggan.'

'Yes. It's an old Pendruggan name,' Piran answered warily, unsure where this was going.

'And you also know the meaning of the name Perran?'

Piran was about to reply testily that of course he knew that too, he was a historian for goodness' sake. But something stopped him.

'It means . . .' He hesitated. 'It means dark one.'

'That it does.' The man turned his face towards Piran. Now he was closer, Piran could see that the man's eyes, while a vibrant if watery blue, were somehow empty – blank – almost soulless.

The man continued: 'Many Ambrose men have been true to their natures. They like to entertain dark thoughts and shun the cosy comforts of life that other men embrace. There's many of the Cornish Ambrose men chose to live alone, refusing family and the company of their fellow men.'

Piran was filled with the urge to defend the Ambrose men, to say that that there were as many who made good lives and loved their wives and their children and were likewise loved in return, but the words refused to come out.

'Let me tell you about this Perran Ambrose that lies here,' the man went on. 'He was a fisherman who worked the waters in and around Pendruggan, lived out on his own in a cottage by the headland. He kept himself to himself; he bothered no one and no one bothered him. Came and sold his fish on the harbour, but pocketed his money and then went 'ome. He wasn't one for alehouses nor merrymaking.'

Piran longed to walk away and to hear no more of this story, but his feet were rooted to the spot. His gaze was locked on the man's eyes, which reflected the flickering lights from the candles.

'One Christmas Eve, there was a terrible shipwreck off the coast; the HMS *Firebrand* was caught in a terrible storm and driven onto the rocks. It was a dreadful night; dead bodies filled the water before being claimed by the waves, but there were many who clung to the wreckage. The villagers heard their cries and brought out their boats, risking their own lives to come to the aid of those in the water, picking them up and bringing them safely to shore, many seemingly more dead than alive. But not Perran Ambrose.'

Here he paused for a moment.

'What did he do?' Piran heard himself ask, though he was almost afraid of the answer.

'He refused to help. Kept his cottage door shut and his boat in harbour, despite desperate entreaties for him to come and help. His fishing boat could have taken many men had he come to their aid; no doubt many more lives would have been saved.'

They were both silent.

'How do you know all this?'

'You won't find everything you need to know inside the pages of a history book!' the man snapped.

How could he possibly know that Piran was an historian?

'After that, the name Ambrose came to mean

something darker in Pendruggan. Perran Ambrose was shunned. No one wanted the fish he brought to harbour. Over time, folks stopped seeing him about. Eventually, they forgot he existed. Then one day he took his boat out and never came back. His body was washed up some time later and he was laid to rest here with no one to mourn him.'

Piran knew that the chill he felt was not merely from the cold air around him. The thought of this man, this Perran Ambrose who shut himself away from life and from his fellow men – who had ceased to care to the extent that he would watch other men drown . . .

'But all that was a long time ago and folks forget.' The man turned once again to Piran and this time he saw something else in those eyes – sorrow? regret?

'They do well to remember and learn the lessons from the past.'

With this, the man turned his back on Piran and the grave of Perran Ambrose and set off down the path away from the church and towards the road.

'But who are you?' Piran shouted after him. 'What is your name?'

The man turned one last time and, as he did so, the lamp he held illuminated a small gold hooped earring in his ear.

Piran's heart froze as the man said, 'They call me Ambrose.'

He watched until the light disappeared into the frozen night air. When at last he turned his eyes up towards the clock, he saw that it was just after midnight. Like a radio being tuned in, the strains of 'Hark the Herald Angels Sing' once more reached his ears. It was almost as if time had stood still.

Piran shook his head, unable to comprehend what had happened.

What could it all mean?

He took another long look at the grave of Perran Ambrose and thought he now understood. Piran knew exactly what he had to do.

*

It was early, not long after 7 a.m. when Piran let himself into Gull's Cry. The house was quiet and still in darkness, though Piran was pleased to see that the nightlight in the hallway was now working, which must mean that the power supply to the village had been restored.

He took off his shoes and his jacket, removed his warm fleece and made his way up the stairs, the ancient floorboards creaking underfoot as he softly opened the door to Helen's spare bedroom, where she lay, fast asleep. He gazed at her for a moment, drinking in her pretty features; she was still youthful and, here, in the half light of dawn, she could almost be a girl of eighteen. His heart swelled with love for her.

The bedroom door let out a creak as it swung closed and Helen stirred. Sitting up in bed it took her a moment to realise that he was standing there.

'Piran, what on earth?'

Before she could say more, he moved quickly to the bed and enveloped her in his arms, kissing her passionately.

He pulled away. 'Please, Helen, don't say anything. I know I've been a miserable old bugger these last weeks and I'm truly sorry. You've got every right never to want to see me again, but I love you, Helen – forgive me?'

She took one look at his open and sincere face and her heart melted. 'Always.'

Folding her arms around his solid frame, she returned his kiss wholeheartedly.

'You're freezing.'

'That's because it's cold out.'

'It's warm in here.'

'Maybe I should get in?'

'Maybe you should. I can think of a couple of ways that you can improve on that apology.'

They had a delicious twenty minutes before they heard the excited chatter of Summer from the other room, wondering if Santa had been to visit. They hurriedly made themselves decent before Terri knocked on the door and she and Summer came to say good morning and Merry Christmas.

Summer threw herself at Piran, who gave her a huge cuddle, enjoying the combined waft of milk and talc that came from her hair and was unique to small children.

'Come on, Summer, let's go downstairs and see what Santa has brought us all,' he said. Then he gave Helen a peck on the cheek, jumped out of bed, grabbed his dressing gown that Helen insisted he keep there and bounded down the stairs.

*

Helen had never seen Piran this excited before. He was like a small kid, eyes shining as he helped Summer to rip open the shiny wrapping paper to get at her presents. There was a wonderful haul and Summer cooed at the sight of the doll's house that he had brought with him.

Helen was touched at the trouble he had taken. 'I had no idea that you were making this, Piran.'

The doll's house was carved in reclaimed beech and Piran had hand-painted it in a soft pink gloss. It was decorated with a climbing wisteria that he had picked out in purple and green paint. He had stayed up all night in the lamplight to finish it.

'It's beautiful. Thank you, Piran.' Helen touched his hand and kissed his cheek.

'I'll make her some furniture too, when she's ready for it.'

After that, he made them all bacon sandwiches and Helen poured glasses of buck's fizz so they could drink a toast.

'Not for me, orange juice will be fine.'

'Are you sure?' Helen looked at him doubtfully. 'It is Christmas.'

'I know that, Helen, more than you realise. Now, drink up. We've got some calls to make.'

*

Within twenty minutes, they had pulled up outside Brown Owl's house, which was on one of the new-build developments just outside the village. Piran rummaged in the back seat of his pickup and pulled out a large cooler box.

'What's in there?'

'A peace offering.'

Moments later, he was standing in front of Brown Owl, apologising profusely for saying uncharitable things about the Brownies' abilities.

'I've brought you something for the Christmas table.' And with this he opened the cooler box, reached inside and pulled out a giant live lobster, which wriggled angrily even though its pincers were secured with elastic bands.

Emma burst out laughing. 'Piran Ambrose! You're an enigma, wrapped in a mystery, wearing a fisherman's jumper – what am I to make of this! Don't think I've ever cooked a lobster before.'

Her children came running out and were full of oohs and ahhs.

'Can we keep him in the fish pond, Mam?' her young son asked.

'And,' added Piran, 'as a further penance, I'll come and take the Brownies through their knots badge.'

'They'll make mincemeat of you!'

All animosity forgotten and with the lobster possibly not even destined for the cooking pot, they climbed back in the car.

'Where to now?' Helen asked.

'Audrey,' Piran answered.

'Ah,' replied Helen. 'She might not be as forgiving as Emma.'

'I'm aware of that. But I've got an idea.'

*

Arriving at Audrey's house, Piran took a deep breath.

'I think I'll stay in the car for this one,' Helen said, and Piran gave her a wink and squeezed her hand.

It took a moment for the door to be answered by Geoffrey, who was attended by two yappy cocker spaniels at his heels, both of which made for Piran's ankles as the door opened, only to be unceremoniously yanked back.

'Get down, boys!' said Geoffrey Tipton, hauling them away before eyeing Piran suspiciously.

'Can I have a word with Audrey, please, Geoff?' he asked meekly.

'I'm not sure she'll want to speak to you,' he sniffed. 'But I'll ask her.'

While Piran spent a nervous few minutes on the doorstep, he turned to look at Helen sitting in the front seat of the pickup with Jack on her knees. She gave him an encouraging smile, but his heart hammered in his chest as Audrey came to the door. Without her battle-dress of tweed coat, headscarf and sensible shoes, she seemed small and fragile in her dressing gown and slippers. Piran felt for the first time that here was someone who was just like everyone else, with the same hopes and fears, but who covered up her vulnerability with an armour of bossiness and bluster.

'Audrey, I—'

'Please make this quick. It is rather cold out here.' She made no move to invite him in.

'I came to tell you that I deeply regret the things I said the other night.'

Audrey regarded him coldly. 'There are things, Mr Ambrose, that once they are said, cannot be unsaid.'

'I appreciate that, Audrey, and I know that you'll find it hard to forgive me. But I want you to know that we all feel . . . I feel . . . that this village wouldn't work without you. You're the oil that keeps the wheels turning and if it wasn't for you, this would be one more Cornish village like many others instead of the special place that we all know Pendruggan is.'

Audrey didn't speak for a moment, but Piran thought, or prayed, that he saw a softening in her eyes.

'Actions speak louder than words, Mr Ambrose.'

'I agree, Audrey, and that's why I'm going to prove it to you. One day a week, I'm going to put myself at your disposal. Whether it's ferrying pensioners to the old folks' lunch or weeding the flower beds on the village green, I'll do whatever you want me to.'

Audrey considered his offer. 'One day a week, you say?'

'I'll make it two!' he added recklessly.

She put her head to one side and after a short pause appeared to make up her mind.

'Very well. But I shall hold you to this – as your word of honour?'

'I won't let you down, Audrey. I promise.'

'Good day to you,' she said, and made to close the door but then added, 'Mr Ambrose . . .'

'Yes, Audrey?'

'A Merry Christmas to you.' She gave him a small smile.

'And a very Merry Christmas to you and Geoff,' he said, returning her smile.

This time, Piran found that he meant every word.

*

'Why, Piran, they're beautiful!'

Simon examined the figurines from the wooden Nativity set that Piran had set down on the steps of the altar. As vicar, he'd been up for a while; Christmas Day was the busiest day of the year for him, but he had a quiet couple of hours before the midday service and then afterwards there would be mulled cider outside the church, drinks in the vicarage and lunch with family and some of the key church helpers.

'I made this years ago for the children in the hospital. Jenna's idea.'

Piran picked up the wooden Baby Jesus in the manger, which he had finished painting in the small hours. 'I thought you could put them under the tree for your Jenna, Simon.'

'Where did you find them?' asked Helen.

'In my shed. When Jenna was killed, nothing else mattered for a long time. And by the time it did, I'd forgotten about these. Until last night.'

He and Helen held each other's gaze for a moment. She squeezed his hand tightly.

'And now?'

'Now they need a new home. Will you take them in, Simon?'

'Nothing would give me greater pleasure.' Simon thought of his own daughter, also called Jenna, and of how her face would light up at the sight of these beautiful figures. 'They'll have pride of place here at the front, where everyone can see them.' He turned his eyes from the manger to his friend. 'And, Piran . . .'

'Yes?'

'Welcome back!'

They exchanged warm smiles.

'Thanks,' said Piran. 'It feels good.'

'Where are you both off to now?'

'Ah!' said Piran mysteriously. 'We are going – and this includes you, Reverend Canter – for a swim. Grab your trunks!'

*

As they left the church, Piran asked Helen to wait for a moment.

'There's one more thing I've got to do. You don't need to come with me.' She gave him a puzzled look, but let him go.

Piran walked towards the churchyard. It seemed different in the weak winter sunshine and he was worried that he wouldn't find what he was looking for. But there it was, in the same place as last night – the final resting place of Perran Ambrose.

Piran knelt before the grave and read the inscription again. He rubbed his eyes and shook his head, unable to believe that what he was seeing was true. But no matter how many times he blinked and read it again, the words were there, literally carved in stone:

Perran Ambrose.
Born 1843. Died 1893 aged fifty.

Below was an inscription:

In loving remembrance of Perran Ambrose who on the twenty-fourth day of December 1893 attended the shipwreck of the HMS Firebrand, which foundered off the coast of Pendruggan.
Perran Ambrose and other Pendruggan men selflessly set out in their fishing boats to rescue as many as they could and toiled for hours in order that they might save those who lay in the water.
A mighty storm raged and while other boats were beaten back, Perran Ambrose continued his quest, though he was thrown from his boat and drowned, but not before many men were saved who owe their lives to his sacrifice.

This headstone was donated by the men and woman of Pendruggan and is dedicated to his memory.

In paradisum deducant te angeli

How could this have changed in one night? Perhaps he had misread the headstone in the darkness, but Piran thought not. Other things had been at work last night and Piran was grateful for the change in his heart and for the new ending for Perran Ambrose. Perhaps it was best if he didn't question events too deeply.

As he turned to leave he spotted a small snowdrop growing in the grass beneath the headstone. It seemed to him a symbol of hope and of new beginnings.

'Rest in peace, Ambrose,' he said gently and made his way back to the car.

*

'You can't be serious – that water is freezing.' Helen and Penny watched, horrified, as Piran and Simon stripped down to their trunks on Shellsand Bay.

Sean, Terri and Summer, along with little Jenna and Simon's family, all marvelled at the throng of people lined up along the shore, eager to see who would win this year's Christmas Day swim.

'Helen, you haven't lived until you've swum out to the buoy on Christmas morning,' Piran said, laughing, jumping up and down to keep warm.

'I'll take your word for it!' she replied, snuggling deeper into her warm fleece-lined coat. She couldn't help thinking that he looked pretty darned good for a man of his age, six-pack still in evidence.

'Piran Ambrose, as I live and breathe!' Don's voice boomed out and he gave his old adversary a slap on the back. Don was now landlord of The Dolphin and was as much a fixture of Pendruggan life as he had always been.

'Don! Not taking part yourself this year, I see?' Don was well wrapped up in winter outdoor gear and Piran could see that he and his wife, Dorrie, were manning the barbecues.

'The days of freezing me bollocks off are well behind me. Think the doctor would have a fit if I even so much as contemplated it

– dodgy ticker and all that.' He tapped his chest with a finger.

'Rubbish, Don. You're scared of the competition – like always.'

After a bit more joshing and banter, there was no time for further chat as Peter, still officiating after all these years though long since retired, rang his bell for the off.

Piran and Simon lined up with the rest of the competitors.

'Remind me why we're doing this, again?' questioned Simon through chattering teeth.

Piran gave him a dazzling smile. 'Because it's Christmas, of course!'

*

To the sound of deafening cheers, Piran raised his pint of Christmas Ale to his lips and took a long, satisfying draw.

'Now that, is pure Ambrosia – excuse the pun!' Piran thought that nothing had ever tasted so good before.

Helen threw her arms around him for the hundredth time.

'I can't believe you won!'

'Neither can I!'

'It was incredible, you were miles ahead of everyone else. How on earth did you do it?'

'I've no idea – perhaps this year I'm just blessed. I feel blessed, anyway.' He gave her a loving kiss on the head and then raised his voice to be heard above the crowd of voices in The Dolphin.

'To make up for being such a grumpy old wanker, I promise that if Audrey will let me, I'll give Pendruggan their best ever Window Twanky in next year's panto!' This news was greeted by whoops and cheers from the whole pub.

'And I'd like to dedicate my win and this wonderful pint of Pendruggan Christmas Ale to all of the Piran Ambroses past, present and future who never forgot and never will forget what goodwill to all men really means.'

He downed his drink. 'Merry Christmas!'

The Beach
CABIN

PROLOGUE

Channel 7 Studios, London, 2000

The floor manager of *Skool's Out*, Channel 7's hit children's TV show, watched the action play out in front of him in a state of high anxiety, rather like a budgerigar left in charge of a cattery, never sure from which direction the danger was going to come from. The programme always went out live at 5.15 p.m. on a Friday and the whole operation was a test of nerves, patience, forbearance and arse-licking for the entire crew. Despite the old show business adage about never working with animals or children, the set was always filled with dozens of hysterical pre-teens, plus that week's line-up of novelty acts. This typically consisted of an assortment of pet dogs that could whine the National Anthem, a nine-year-old who could fart at the same decibel level as a car horn and some idiot intent on breaking a silly world record, like how many times you can kick your own butt in one minute. On top of this the crew had to contend with the fragile egos and sometimes ridiculous demands of the celebrity guests, combined with the inflated ones of the show's presenters. Anything could go wrong, and it was a fine balance between giving the show's trademark anarchy full flight while keeping things under control.

The set was designed to look like a school where the kids had taken over. Walls were daubed in graffiti, there were 'detention' cells that the guests could be placed in if they displeased the 'kids' and everything had a slightly sinister quality that was pitched some-where between St Trinian's and a Tim Burton movie.

The floor manager heard the director's voice from the control room through his earpiece. 'Dave and cameras move over to the cell area for Robbie's detention skit.'

'Yep.' On the set, Robbie Williams had been placed in one of the cells and was being lambasted by the show's irreverent star, a puppet called Brian the Cat – a mass of tatty black-and-white fur and Denis Healey eyebrows who spoke in the thick Mancunian tones of his puppeteer. Brian was lambasting Robbie from outside his cell accompanied by his side-kick, a young presenter called Kirsty.

'Robbie Williams, the studio audience have unanimously decided to give you detention on account of not only crimes against music . . .'

The audience howled with laughter.

'. . . but also, for eating all the pies!'

Cue more hysterical screaming.

Ed Appleby, the studio runner, watched tensely from his position behind the camera crew. He could see Robbie's PA and his publicity manager watching stony-faced from the wings. If things went too far and Robbie got upset, there would be hell to pay. Ed took his *Joe 90* glasses off, gave them a quick wipe before putting them back on and then ran his hand anxiously through his dark curly hair.

Brian the Cat was egging the audience on. 'What do you reckon? Shall we let him go home now, kids? Has he done his detention?'

'Splat him!' the children screamed. Robbie

grabbed the cell bars and shook his head vigorously, mouthing something Ed couldn't hear over the roaring of the audience, but which looked suspiciously like, *Bollocks to that.*

'Let him have it!' declared Brian triumphantly, and a bucket that had been hovering above Robbie's head tipped over and released a yellow goo over his head.

'Camera one, zoom in,' said the director over talkback.

The camera zoomed in to see Robbie's expression as the yellow gunk slicked down his face and chest.

Robbie wiped the gunk away from his eyes with his fingers and licked his lips. There was an anxious pause in the room before Robbie said in his soft Northern accent, 'Mmmn, lemon curd, nice. Can I have a jar to take back to me mam, sir?'

As the audience cheered their raucous approval, Ed saw the faces of Robbie's people relax.

The camera moved away to Kirsty. 'Ha-ha! Now let's see the new video from 5ive – they're going to be here next week and we're going to give them a proper *Skool's Out* welcome, aren't we?'

Ed's shoulders relaxed briefly, but they immediately tensed again as he felt someone sidle up to him and gently pinch his bottom. He turned sharply and was immensely relieved to see Charlotte Finney, the show's design director, standing next to him. They were virtually the same age, but, while Ed was still working his way up the ranks as a lowly junior, Charlotte was responsible not only for the way the show looked, but also the tone and feel. All the senior managers took her seriously, though, judging from her expression, she was feeling anything but serious. She gave him a cheeky wink.

'Thank God it's you!'

'Who else were you expecting to make contact with your sexy arse, Ed?' she said huskily.

'God knows in this madhouse,' he whispered back. 'I'd better go.'

There would now be a brief three-minute video interlude for everyone to get to their new place, make a quick costume change and prepare for the next segment.

Ed shot Charlotte a look that said *sorry* and raced over to release Robbie from his temporary cell. A posse of Robbie's people and studio assistants followed hot on his heels, bringing hot towels and clean clothes for the star. Declining their offers of help, Robbie took off his T-shirt and used it to wipe away the yellow slime while flaunting his taut and tanned six-pack.

'Keith, you fucker, I'll get you back for that!' he said good-naturedly to Brian's puppeteer, Keith Puckley, who had extricated himself from Brian's undercarriage.

'Didn't they tell you at stage school that this would happen, Rob?' Brian shot back.

'Fuck off!' Robbie grinned, and playfully poked Keith's middle-aged paunch. 'Who ate all the pies, eh? I think we know the answer to that one!'

'Must mean I'm in with a chance as your replacement in Take That – give your mate Gary Barlow a call and tell him I'm free.'

Before they could trade further insults, Ed interjected: 'Keith, you're not free yet – Brian has to judge the burping competition in one minute. Robbie, we need to get you cleaned up for the finale. You're singing us out with "Rock DJ".'

'Oh yeah, ace.' With a final grin at Keith,

Robbie headed off to make-up, entourage of flunkies in tow.

Ed and Keith looked at each other. Only another thirty agonising minutes to go, then they could all breathe out.

*

An hour and a half later, Robbie had been dispatched in his limo, the kids had all been loaded on the coaches that would take them home to Milton Keynes or wherever it was they had come from, and Ed was sitting on the steps at the rear entrance of Channel 7's Soho studios, smoking a crafty cigarette. The doors behind him opened with a crash as Keith, still accompanied by Brian the Cat, emerged. The puppet was operated from below with a combination of levers and sticks, which allowed his limbs to function. Brian's head and body lolled lifeless over Keith's arm.

'Thank fuck that's over for another week,' said Keith with feeling as he plonked himself down on the step next to Ed. 'I'm getting too old for all this shit.'

'Rubbish,' said Ed. 'The show wouldn't work without Brian. You love it, you know you do.'

Keith grunted something unintelligible in reply, lighting up his cigarette and pulling heavily on it.

The back door opened again and Charlotte stepped out. He wasn't aware of it, but Ed's face lit up as if it had been illuminated by a thousand-watt light bulb. Charlotte was dressed in green army combat trousers and a fitted black T-shirt that showed just a hint of her soft creamy belly when she lifted her arms up. Her choppy, layered red hair, probably a shade of red that didn't occur in nature, framed her oval face and made her green eyes greener. Charlotte had told Ed that she was actually a blonde, but he didn't care. He thought she was utterly gorgeous.

'Keith Puckley, put that cigarette out now!' She pointed at Keith accusingly. 'If Brian gets a fag burn it'll be Muggins here that'll have to sit up all night stitching him, or, God forbid, making another one from scratch – which I've already had to do once, thanks to the Christmas party shenanigans.'

'Sorry, Charlotte,' said Keith meekly. 'I was gasping.'

'Oh, all right, but be careful.' Charlotte softened and ruffled Brian's fur affectionately. 'God knows why, but I've become attached to the horrible little bastard.'

'You wouldn't want to be as attached to him as I am. Feel like I can't get away from the little bugger,' he said gloomily.

Charlotte patted his arm sympathetically. 'Maybe it's time to put Brian back in his box, Keith. It's been a long day.'

'You're probably right.' Keith stubbed out his cigarette and stood up. 'Time to go home.'

As he departed he said, 'And no getting up to any hanky-panky, you two. I might be an old duffer but I don't miss much.'

Ed and Charlotte tried to look innocent. 'I don't know what you mean, Keith,' Charlotte said, trying to stop a grin from spreading over her face.

'A likely story.' He wished them goodnight and headed inside.

After a moment, once she was sure he'd gone, Charlotte inched closer to Ed so that their thighs were touching. Her hand crept under the back of his T-shirt and she leaned in to nibble his ear.

Ed's senses felt under assault; she smelled of fresh meadow flowers and Ed could feel the swell of her breasts against his chest. It took all his willpower not to reach under her T-shirt and slip his hand under her bra. Despite this, it was Ed who pulled away first.

'We'd better be careful, someone might see us.'

Charlotte slipped her hand into his. 'They all know already. Look at Keith – and he's well out of the gossip loop.'

'No.' Ed shook his head. 'They don't know. Not officially, anyway, and I don't think they should, not yet. We've talked about this.'

She pulled away and looked at him with a frown. 'Yes, we might have talked about it, but I still don't see we have anything to hide.'

Ed squeezed her hand and tried to make light of it. 'I know you don't, but you're the design director and I'm the lowly runner. They'll think I'm trying to sleep my way to the top.' He tried to engage her with a smile.

Charlotte's frown deepened. 'I don't care what they think. We've been seeing each other for nearly a year. Your toothbrush can't remember what your bathroom looks like, I let your best friend sleep on my sofa for three weeks and I've played in a Scrabble contest with your mum. For heaven's sake, Ed, we couldn't be more together if we tried.'

'But you know what the top brass are like. They hate relationships on set in case things go wrong.'

'What's going to go wrong?' Charlotte looked alarmed.

'Nothing! Nothing's going to go wrong, Charlotte. But I'm building my career, and yours is going so well. We don't want anything to spoil that, do we?'

Ed felt as though the conversation was running away from him but couldn't work out where he'd gone wrong. This was the first time Charlotte had ever said anything about wanting their relationship to be more open. They'd both been happy for their work and personal lives to be separate – hadn't they?

He pulled his cigarettes from his top pocket, took one for himself and offered one to Charlotte. She shook her head, her lips set in a thin line.

'I've given up.'

'Since when?'

'This morning.'

'Oh?'

Ed removed the cigarette from his mouth unlit. Charlotte was looking at him, an unreadable expression on her face. It wasn't a look he recognised or that he felt particularly comfortable with, if he was honest.

'What's wrong, Charlotte?'

Charlotte tugged at her long fringe, something he'd noticed she did when she was nervous or anxious.

'Something's happened.'

When he thought about it later, Ed realised what she said next was literally the last thing he'd have thought she was going to say. He'd have been less surprised if she'd told him she'd been born with a penis and had undergone a sex change.

'I'm pregnant.'

That she uttered these words and not some others was his justification for his response, though he knew as soon as the words left his mouth that it was completely the wrong thing to say in the circumstances.

'Oh, shit!'

Charlotte immediately stiffened, eyed him with a look that seemed to communicate both disappointment and distress, and snatched her hand away from his.

'Oh, shit!' he said again, unable to absorb what those two words could mean for both of them. Registering the look in her eyes, he panicked. 'I didn't mean oh, shit, I meant oh, no. I mean, it's the timing, isn't it, for both of us.' Unable to stop himself, he blathered on: 'Your job, mine . . . I always thought we'd get together properly one day – you know, married, kids and all that – but just not now . . .'

This was all coming out wrong. He looked at Charlotte, his secret girlfriend . . . beautiful, clever Charlotte . . . the mother of his children . . .

At this thought, a little spark seemed to ignite somewhere inside him and for a moment he saw them, his future family, and words and feelings that he'd never recognised in himself flickered within him: father, husband, protector . . .

But Charlotte was getting up off the step, moving towards the door. She reached for the handle, then paused to look back at him. 'The traditional response when someone announces they're expecting a baby is "Congratulations!" Look, we'll talk about it later, Ed. You're right, my timing is shit.'

'Wait, Charlotte!' He leapt up and reached for her, but she brushed his hand away.

'Look, Ed, it's fine. We'll talk later. Right now I need to go home.'

As Ed watched her retreating back and scrabbled to his feet to catch her, he knew he'd screwed it up big time. If this was a test, then he had failed miserably.

He only hoped it wasn't too late and she'd give him a chance to make things right.

1

Pendruggan, Cornwall, 2015

Penny Leighton was sitting in the kitchen of the Old Vicarage with her feet up on the kitchen table – it was her table, after all – enjoying a freshly poured cup of tea. For once the house was quiet: her husband had gone over to the church hall, where he was hosting the Pendruggan Mother and Toddlers' Group as part of his vicarly duties. Across the table, Ed Appleby hunched over a laptop, wrinkling his brow as he perused stately homes on his web browser.

'That list Cassie sent over of possible locations for Lady Arundell's family pile – I've worked my way through and eliminated the ones that wouldn't be suitable. Lanhydrock would be ideal, but I also like the sound of

Prideaux Place, smaller but gorgeous. It's not far from here and apparently it has amazing grounds overlooking Padstow. As we've got a break in filming, maybe I should arrange a meeting with the owners, do a recce – what do you think, Pen?'

When his question went unanswered, Ed looked over the top of his laptop. The producer of *The Mr Tibbs Mysteries* seemed oblivious to his presence. She had just dunked a HobNob in her tea before popping it into her mouth and was currently savouring the soft, sugary crunch. A look of sheer bliss on her face, she let out a long 'mmmm'.

Ed took off his thick-rimmed Michael Caine glasses and rubbed at his tired eyes. 'Did you hear any of that, Pen?'

'You know, without your glasses on you look about seventeen.' Penny dunked another corner of her biscuit into her tea.

'Don't change the subject.'

'Why not? Why do we have to talk about work? We've four weeks' enforced break while our leading lady goes off and does her one-woman thing at the Old Vic. What's wrong with spending a morning eating HobNobs and taking it easy for once?' She cast a longing gaze at the copy of *Grazia* lying unopened by her side.

Mr Tibbs, based on the novels of Mavis Carew and filmed on location in the picturesque Cornish seaside village where Penny had made her home, had proved to be such a runaway success that they were now halfway through filming the fourth series. The invasion of the cast and crew, and the transformation of Pendruggan into something straight out of the 1930s, had become an annual fixture in the village calendar. Some of the locals had been resistant, but most welcomed the film crew, especially now that the series had put Pendruggan on the tourist map. Queenie's shop had become a must-see destination for the holidaymakers who flooded the village each summer.

Ed sighed and shut his laptop.

'Besides,' Penny added, 'it's not your job to sort out locations. Cassie's already done half the work. Let *her* go and see them. She's more than capable. You can make your decision once she's written up her recommendations.'

'I'm the location manager. It's my job.'

'Cassie's the assistant location manager, and that makes it *her* job. It's called delegating, Ed. Anyway, you look exhausted.'

'I am exhausted.'

'Then go home and try to put your feet up for a while. Spend some time with Charlotte and those gorgeous children of yours. You all look like something out of a Boden advert.'

Ed let out a humourless laugh. 'Looks can be deceptive, Pen.'

Penny put down her cuppa and leaned closer.

'What's the matter, Ed? You and I have worked on umpteen productions together over the years. I've seen you go from junior runner on *Blue Peter* to location manager on a Woody Allen movie, and, no matter how demanding the job, you've shown up for work full of enthusiasm and energy. I've never seen you out of sorts – until now. You're usually so cheerful – *too* bloody cheerful, in fact!'

'But it hasn't affected my work?' he asked anxiously. 'Has anyone said anything?'

'No of course not. Don't be silly.' She batted away his anxiety with a wave of her hand. 'No one's noticed a thing. Except me, and that's only because we've known each other such a long time.'

Ed wiped his glasses clean on the corner of his Superdry T-shirt and let out a sigh.

'Oh, I don't know . . .' He hesitated, wondering how to articulate what he was feeling without making it sound melodramatic. 'Alex has been a bit difficult lately. She's not been herself and Charlotte's worried something's up at school.'

'She's fifteen,' Penny reasoned. 'They're unknowable at that age. You and Charlotte are there for her, though. You're solid, right?'

Solid, thought Ed. Before all this had happened he wouldn't have hesitated to say yes. They both adored the kids and put their needs first. For Ed that involved taking on work that meant they could leave London and buy a large house on the seafront in Worthing, and cover school fees so that both kids got the best education possible, plus a bit left over for long summer holidays in the South of France so they could spend time as a family. For Charlotte it had meant giving up work until the kids started school. Then she had become involved with a local theatre group, helping out with set design – always fitting it around the children's needs, because Ed wasn't around to help as much as he would like. In order to command the big salary he had to spend large chunks of time away on location. The last couple of years, he seemed to have spent most of his time at the opposite end of the country to Charlotte and the kids.

'I think so,' he replied, trying hard to keep the uncertainty out of his voice. 'Charlotte says I'm away too much.'

'Are you?'

'Perhaps, but only the last year or so. You know how it is in this business, Pen. Projects are tied up years ahead, you sign your life away.'

'You're one of the best in the business, Ed. You can pick and choose your projects now.'

'I'm not so sure. People have short memories.'

'Only for people they want to forget.'

Ed laughed at this. 'Point taken.'

But the thing that was really worrying him was the one thing he couldn't bring himself to tell Penny. Over the past year the distance between him and Charlotte had been growing, and it was a distance that had nothing to do with being at opposite ends of the country. They always used to make the most of the weeks when he was at home, but now Charlotte seemed to spend every minute she could at the theatre. Worse still, she'd taken to sleeping in the spare room, citing his fidgeting in bed as the reason. 'I've got used to sleeping without you, Ed,' she'd told him bluntly.

Ed felt sure there was more to it. Whatever their ups and downs over the years, the two of them had always been physically close. It made this new distance between them all the more painful. Then four weeks ago, during his last stay at home, he'd waited until Charlotte had gone to take a bath before sneaking into the spare bedroom and picking up her phone. Though he hated himself for it, he clicked on her inbox and scrolled through the messages. Among them he found one that made his heart stop. It was a text message from Henry, the director at the theatre. He could hardly bear to think about the words he'd seen: *I love you . . . can't live without you . . .*

The thought that his wife was in love with someone else tore at his insides. He pushed it away.

'Look,' said Penny, pulling him back to the present, 'what you need is a break. Why don't you bring them all down here for the weekend? One of the cottages in the village is for rent. It's recently been bought by some second-homers who're letting it out when they aren't here. It would be perfect for you and the family, and the best thing about it is that it's got this amazing beach cabin on Shellsand Bay that comes as part of the package.'

'How do you know it's available?'

'Queenie told me. The owners have engaged her as their key holder. I can easily get their number off her.' Penny picked up her phone and started to call Queenie.

'Hang on, I'm not sure. I'd need to check with Charlotte – they might have plans.'

'Ed, stop procrastinating. You need to spend some time with your family and that's that.'

Ed did as he was told. Now that the idea was in his head he ached to see his kids. The last four weeks he'd avoided going home, citing complications with the production. Anything rather than confront the situation and risk Charlotte telling him that she no longer loved him, that their marriage was over.

Maybe Penny was right. They hadn't been seeing enough of each other, that was all. He'd been letting his imagination run riot. Yes, they could sort this all out – a little holiday was exactly what they needed.

*

'Please can you get off my foot, Molly?' Charlotte looked down into the soft adoring eyes of their bearded collie. Molly was a shaggy-coated four-year-old, absolutely enormous and intent on getting as close as she could to Charlotte, which meant that crushed toes were part and parcel of being a dog owner in the Appleby household.

Charlotte eyed the ingredients in front of her. Prawns in their shells. Coconut milk. Now what else was it that Nigel Slater had said should go in? The recipe had been in the *Observer* at the weekend, but she'd forgotten to tear it out before chucking the paper into

the recycling box. She'd decided to give it a
go anyway, hoping that she could rely on
her memory. A green curry – would that be
Indian? Or Sri Lankan? She rummaged in
the cupboard and fished out some curry
powder. What else? There'd been a green herb
of some sort . . . And was it a lemon or a
lime he used? She went to the fridge: there
was no lime, so it would have to be lemon,
and the only green herb she could see was a
slightly withered stalk of parsley. That'd do.
Maybe chuck in a carrot or two? And mangetout – she had plenty of mangetout and it
was definitely one of Nigel's ingredients.

Any other evening Charlotte would have
abandoned all thought of making the dish as
soon as she discovered the recipe was lost,
but tonight she was glad of the challenge. She
needed something to distract her from the
worries racing through her mind. Alex should
have been home an hour ago. They'd agreed
that she could go to her best friend Poppy's
house for the afternoon, provided she was
home by seven. When seven thirty rolled
around with no sign of her daughter and no
word of explanation, Charlotte had tried

to ring her, but an automated announcement informed her that the person she was calling was not available. So she rang Poppy's mum to ask her to send Alex on her way – only to discover that Alex hadn't been there in days. Fighting the urge to panic and ring all three emergency services and run up and down the street in hysteria, she'd focused on remaining calm and waiting it out. It wasn't the first time Alex had disappeared for a few hours with no explanation. It had been less obvious during term time, though Charlotte had managed to catch her out a few times, but now the holidays were here it was clear that Alex was going somewhere she didn't want anyone else to know about.

There had been none of the usual telltale signs of a boyfriend. No dreamy looks over the breakfast table, or furtive late-night phone calls. Charlotte wasn't much of a snoop, so she could be wrong, but in her experience boy trouble usually came with bells on, shouting its presence loud and clear. No, this felt like something else. Perhaps if she'd been around a bit more, then Alex would have opened up to her. But she'd been preoccupied with everything that was happening with Henry – she'd be lying to herself if she didn't admit to taking her eye off the ball.

Charlotte proceeded to chop up all the ingredients with more confidence than she felt. The resulting mix looked nowhere near as lovely as the photos of Nigel's efforts . . .

She lit the flame under the deep sauté pan and threw in the vegetables. Behind her she heard the front door shut quietly in the hallway and turned with great relief to see her daughter Alex slipping past the kitchen door in the direction of the stairs.

'Hi, darling,' she called out.

Alex's foot stopped on the stairs. 'Hi, Mum.'

'Got a minute?'

Silence, but then, a moment later, the slow plod of reluctant footsteps back down the hall. Alex's hair had been purple when she'd first dyed it, but it had now faded to a lilacy-blue and was scraped back in a ponytail. Charlotte missed her daughter's natural copper-blonde hair but hoped it would stage a return one day. Chewing the toggle of her hoodie, Alex hovered by the door.

'Been somewhere nice?' Charlotte asked

casually. *Must avoid an argument*, she told herself. *Tread carefully.*

'I was at Poppy's, I told you.'

Damn. Why do you have to lie, Alex? Why can't you tell me where you've been?

'I'm making dinner. Are you hungry?' she asked, a touch too brightly.

'No, thanks. We had KFC.'

We? Who's 'we'?

'What is it?'

Good question. 'It's a prawn curry. Nigel Slater.'

Alex rolled her eyes. 'Why don't you just stick to ready meals, Mum?'

'I like cooking.' It was true.

'But you're not very good at it.'

'I shall ignore your implied insult. I've been complimented on my cooking, I'll have you know.'

'Only by Granny Alice, who lost her taste buds when a bomb fell on her house during the war.'

'Not only Granny Alice, actually: many people.'

'Yeah, right, Mum,' Alex replied sceptically, turning to leave.

Charlotte was on the verge of letting her go, but then decided it was time to bite the bullet and confront her daughter. 'Alex, I called Poppy's mum when you were late home. She said—'

Alex's explosive response took Charlotte by surprise, even though she'd been exposed to enough teen anger that she ought to be used to it by now. 'How dare you! You're always snooping around and following me. Why can't you let me live my own life?'

'Alex, darling, I don't want to interfere, but you're only fifteen and we worry about your safety, that's all.'

'Rubbish! You just want to control me.'

Charlotte struggled to keep her voice even. 'Alex, I understand how—'

'No, you don't! You can never know how it feels to be me!' And, with this, Alex raced out of the room and up the stairs, slamming her bedroom door behind her.

Charlotte looked at Molly, who was cowering under the pine kitchen table. 'Well, that went as well as can be expected,' she muttered, and Molly crept out and sat on her foot again, giving her hand a consoling lick. 'Thanks,

Molly. I can always rely on you to be here for me.'

If only she could say the same of her husband. Charlotte silently cursed Ed for never being home when he was needed. Instead, he was hundreds of miles away as usual while she held the fort at home, though it felt very much like a battle she was fast losing.

He was so much better with Alex than she was; he always knew how to bring her round. Part of the problem was that she and Alex were too much alike: spiky, emotional rather than rational, prone to keeping secrets . . . But the old Alex had hated confrontation. On the rare occasions when she did get in an argument, she was always the one who would try to make up. The familiar gnawing guilt fluttered in her belly, berating her. *This is your fault. If you weren't spending so much time at the theatre . . . All that time with Henry when you should be at home . . .*

As if on cue, her phone rang. It was Ed. *Hello, stranger*, she thought.

'Hi, Ed. How's it going?'

'Yeah, good. We're finished now for four

weeks – Dahlia's gone off to do her one-woman show in London.'

'Oh, God, that! What's it about again?'

'Um, not sure – something to do with older people having a lot of sex?'

'Crikey.'

'Kids OK?'

'You probably know better than I do.'

Whenever he was away, Ed kept in daily contact with them by text and FaceTime.

There was a pause at the other end of the line. She could picture him floundering over what to say next without putting his foot in it.

'I was wondering,' he said eventually, 'how would it be if you all came down to Pendruggan for a few days? There's a great place we can stay – it's right by the beach. We haven't seen much of each other over the last few weeks—'

'Months, more like. And whose fault is that?' Charlotte couldn't stop the words slipping out.

'I know, I know.' Ed's voice sounded pained. 'But I think it would be good for the kids – and for us.'

'I'm not sure, Ed.' Charlotte knew from

experience what a holiday could be like when Ed was in work mode. 'You couldn't find time to join us in France last month. Apart from one long weekend when you deigned to make an appearance, I had to hold the fort with my mum and dad. And those few days you *were* there you spent on your laptop or iPad, working. And when you weren't working you were sleeping – or drinking too much.'

There was silence from the other end of the line. Charlotte was already regretting her outburst and was on the verge of apologising and explaining why she'd felt the need to vent when Ed suddenly blurted, 'Please, Charlotte, I promise I'll be totally "there". No phones, no laptop, no iPad. Just us. We need this.'

Charlotte breathed in deeply. 'Let me think about it and call you back. Alex is being tricky at the moment, and, even at the best of times, getting the kids to do anything outside their comfort zone is practically impossible. Besides, Pendruggan is a good five-hour drive, and—'

'It'll be worth it,' Ed pleaded. 'I promise you – come on, let's do it.'

Still Charlotte wouldn't cave in. Promising that she'd call him back once she'd spoken to the kids, she hung up the phone and eyed the contents of the saucepan. It hadn't looked like this in the *Observer*. She pulled the ring on the tin of coconut milk and hoped for the best.

*

Charlotte knocked on Sam's door and popped her head in. Her eleven-year-old was sprawled across his bed watching a YouTube video on his iPad.

'Dinnertime.'

'What is it?' he asked, without looking up.

Charlotte looked down at the gloopy rice-and-sauce concoction on the tray she had brought up. 'Prawn surprise.'

Sam raised his head and frowned at her. 'Is a prawn something you want to be surprised by?'

'That's a very good question, Sam. Perhaps we're about to find out the answer.'

She sat next to him on the bed and he scrutinised the contents of the tray. Taking the beaker of milk, he took a long slurp and said, 'Can I have a burger in a bun?'

Charlotte looked down sadly at the prawn surprise. 'Would Birds Eye be an acceptable option for you, sir?'

'Perfectly splendid, m'dear.' And Sam finished off the milk and replaced the beaker on the tray with a flourish.

'What's that you're watching?' Charlotte asked.

'This is the most amazing thing ever, Mum. It's Spike Turner, the skateboard pro. He's doing this totally awesome bitchslap.'

'Sam!'

'Don't be lame, Mum – it's skate lingo.' For the next five minutes Sam gave her an incomprehensible commentary that consisted of terms like *nollie*, *lipslide* and *mongo*. She tried to keep up but most of it went over her head.

'Sam,' she ventured when at last there was a brief lull in his analysis, 'how would you feel about a little trip?'

'Where to?'

A voice behind them said, 'Cornwall. To see Dad.'

They both turned to see Alex standing in Sam's doorway holding her phone. 'I talked to him already – he called to tell me about it.'

That was crafty, thought Charlotte. As always, he'd managed to get Alex on side. The mood she was in earlier, it must have taken a major charm offensive to win her over.

'So, what do you think?'

'I want to go. I haven't seen Dad for ages.'

Charlotte look at Sam. 'What about you?'

Sam barely glanced away from Spike's latest heelflip. 'Dunno. Have they got wi-fi?'

'Yes,' said Alex. 'I checked that with Dad.'

'Cool,' said Sam. 'Then I can show Dad Spike's video.'

Feeling that she was losing control of the decision-making process, Charlotte chimed in: 'Hang on a minute. There's no way I'm going to drive all the way to Cornwall for the weekend so that the pair of you can sit watching YouTube or texting your friends the whole time. I want us to do things as a family, otherwise we might as well stay here.'

The children both shrugged. 'OK,' they said in unison.

'It's a bloody long drive, too, so we'll have to be up and ready to go by six a.m. And I'm not doing all the packing by myself – you'll both have to help.'

'OK.'

'And we have to make it a proper break, be a family, do things together.'

'OK!'

'Even if it means not being glued to your iPad for the next three days?'

'OK! *OK!*'

*

As Charlotte scraped the untouched prawn surprise into Molly's bowl she wondered at the ease with which the children had agreed to come. Maybe this trip was something that needed to happen. If nothing else, it would give her and Ed a chance to have a proper talk, clear the air. They'd been dancing around each other for too long.

As Molly sniffed noncommittally at her bowl, Charlotte picked up her phone. She'd text Ed later. First she needed to call Henry . . .

2

It was gone 9.30 a.m. and Charlotte was only now switching on the satnav.

'Mum!' whined Sam from the back seat. 'Why does it have to be me in the back with Molly?'

'I've told you, Sam, you can swap seats with Alex halfway through. Now let me concentrate on putting this postcode in the satnav so we can get going. I was hoping to miss the worst of the traffic, but we're so late—'

'It was you who overslept, Mum,' Alex pointed out smugly.

Charlotte cast an irritated glance at her daughter, sitting in the passenger seat fiddling with her headphones.

'That's because I was up past midnight, packing.'

'You love your bed too much, Mum.'

'It *is* the holidays.' Charlotte wasn't sure why she needed to justify herself. She and the children were all good sleepers. It was Ed who tossed and turned, often padding downstairs in the middle of the night, dogged with insomnia brought on by worries about work.

'Mum!' Sam nudged the back of her seat with his knee. 'Why do I have to get stuck with Molly?'

Charlotte turned to look at Molly. The expression 'hangdog' could have been coined especially for her. Molly's head was hung low and her soulful eyes gazed out mournfully from under her shaggy hair.

'Poor old Mol,' Charlotte cooed sympathetically. 'You totally hate car travel, don't you, girl?' And she reached out to stroke her. Molly responded by giving her hand a sorrowful lick, then put her head down on her paws with a sigh.

'Nobody gave her any food, did they?' Charlotte asked suspiciously.

'No,' they both answered, but Charlotte thought that Sam looked shifty.

'Sam?'

'Nothing, I promise!' he protested.

'Well, if Molly gets sick,' she warned, 'I'll have a pretty good idea why. Now, let's get this show on the road.'

'Hang on, Mum,' Alex said suddenly, rummaging in her bag. 'I've forgotten my charger.'

'Alex!'

'What! You were rushing me!'

'Oh, just hurry up, will you.' She thrust the door key at Alex, who leapt from the car and ran towards the house. Shaking her head, Charlotte returned her gaze to the satnav, which had just finished calibrating. The estimated journey time popped up on screen: five hours and seven minutes. *Great*, thought Charlotte, *this is going to be* so *much fun*.

Adjusting the rear-view mirror, Charlotte caught sight of herself and pushed her long fringe behind her ear. Her short, layered hairstyle hadn't changed much over the years, though the spicy copper colour was a thing of the past. Charlotte's naturally light-blonde hair was now flecked with grey, which she disguised with highlights. The smattering of freckles over her nose and cheeks gave her a girlish appearance, but there was no ignoring the crow's feet and laughter lines that were becoming more prominent with every passing year. It didn't bother her unduly: getting older was better than the alternative, she always thought.

Alex dashed back to the car and thrust the door keys at her mother. 'Did you lock up?'

'Yes.'

'Double-locked it?'

'Yes, Mum. Let's go!'

'Right, A303, here we come. Oh, by the way, we're going to make a little stop en route . . .'

*

'Where are we going, Mum?'

Two hours in and Alex had finally taken off her headphones. Sam was dozing on the back seat.

'Well . . .' Charlotte said enthusiastically, 'I thought we'd stop at Stonehenge.'

'Why?'

'It's sort of on the way, and you and Sam have never seen it, and I haven't been there for years. And . . . why not? We're on holiday, aren't we? We said we'd do things as a family – and you promised there'd be no grumbling.'

'Don't remember promising that,' Sam mumbled under his breath from the back.

'It's a bit random, Mum.' Alex raised her eyes heavenward.

'No, it isn't.' Charlotte was conscious of the defensive tone in her voice. She was wondering now what had possessed her. As much for her own benefit as the children's, she tried to explain why she felt the need to make this detour: 'Stonehenge is an amazing place. I came here when I was a kid, but couldn't remember anything about it, so I asked your dad to bring me here once when it was the summer solstice. I was pregnant with you at the time.'

'Really?' Alex sounded genuinely interested for once.

'Yep. So, technically, you've been here too.'

'Cool.'

Charlotte stole a glance at her daughter. Alex had Ed's nose and his eyes and his brown wavy hair. Sam took after her with his fair hair and skin.

'What were you listening to? On your phone?'

Alex shrugged. 'One of my Spotify playlists.'

'Oh, like those ones that you and Poppy used to spend hours putting together in the kitchen?'

'It's not one of those,' Alex said tetchily.

'Oh.' It suddenly struck Charlotte that she couldn't remember the last time Poppy had been round to the house. The two girls had been best friends ever since primary school and had made the leap to senior school together. For years they'd been inseparable, wearing the same clothes, liking the same films and music and TV shows, and even sounding alike. But, apart from Alex telling Charlotte that she'd been with Poppy when she hadn't, there'd been no mention of her for ages. Charlotte could have kicked herself for not realising that Poppy hadn't been on the scene for a while. Perhaps she'd give Carol, Poppy's mum, a call and ask her about it, though Alex would go nuts if she found out she was snooping.

'Stick it on the Bluetooth and let's have a listen? I could do with waking up. So could Rip Van Winkle back there.' Charlotte nodded towards Sam in the back seat. 'We'll be at Stonehenge soon.'

Alex paused as if weighing her options, then gave another shrug and connected her phone to the Bluetooth. A moment later a playlist popped up on the screen of the car's media player: 'Lily's Love List'. The first track came through the speakers, it was 'Stay with Me' by Sam Smith.

'Who's Lily?' Charlotte asked.

Alex stiffened. 'No one.'

'No one called Lily?'

'She's just one of the girls at school,' Alex said through gritted teeth.

Clearly, the question had hit a raw nerve, but Charlotte had no idea why. Who was this girl? And, if the two of them were friendly enough to be sharing playlists, why hadn't Alex brought her home?

Charlotte put the questions to one side for a moment as she sang along with Sam's lonesome sentiments, but, the moment she did, Alex clicked on her phone and stopped the track.

'Why did you turn it off? I was enjoying that.'

'You were ruining it! Can't you put your Happy Mondays CD on like you normally do.'

All right all right, thought Charlotte, *don't get your knickers in a twist*. She popped the CD in. The last thing she wanted was to infuriate her touchy daughter even further.

*

The car pulled up on the roadside and the three of them looked at the 4,500-year-old monument. A light rain was falling and the ancient site sat behind a wire fence, cloaked in drizzle. Charlotte couldn't help thinking that they weren't seeing the place at its best.

'What do you think? Hordes of slaves dragged those stones across the country to get them here, you know.'

There was a moment's silence before Alex said, 'It's smaller than I thought it would be.'

'Yeah, it's puny,' Sam agreed.

'It's quite big, actually. It's just that people have these preconceptions . . .'

'Yes,' Sam said flatly. 'Preconceptions that it's bigger and better than it actually is.'

Charlotte tutted at his lack of appreciation. 'Well, the last time I came—'

'*We* came,' corrected Alex.

'The last time *we* came it was amazing,' she persevered.

Charlotte could remember the day so vividly. She'd been eaten up with anxiety. Her pregnancy had been going well, she was fit and healthy and her midwife was pleased with how things were progressing, yet she couldn't help feeling overwhelmed at what was to come. She decided that what she needed was something to ground her, something to remind her that childbirth was part of the endless cycle of life and not merely something to scare the shit out of you. She'd always liked to dabble in alternative stuff. Ed used to tease her about it, saying she was a bit 'woo-woo', but she didn't care. A lot of it was mumbo-jumbo, but you couldn't argue with the magical antiquity of a place like Stonehenge.

The summer solstice was approaching and she'd told Ed that she wanted to see the sun rise at Stonehenge, never expecting that he would embrace the idea. But he surprised her by offering to drive them there, and he'd even booked them into a B&B somewhere close the night before so she wouldn't be too tired to appreciate it. As they ate a pub meal on the eve of the longest day of the year, Charlotte could hear the locals discussing the approaching event.

'Only them druids is all that's allowed on the site now,' said an ancient barfly as he supped his pint.

Curious, as they got up to leave Charlotte

asked him whether they would be allowed to join the ceremony.

'No, my love, they don't let anyone 'cept druids come to the stones these days. Too many New Age travellers and the like spoiling the site, they reckon.'

Charlotte was bitterly disappointed that she wouldn't be able to get close enough to touch the stones and feel the connection between herself and the baby growing inside her with something timeless, enduring and powerful.

But, at 4 a.m., Ed had woken her gently and told her to wrap up in warm clothes. She didn't know how he'd found out about it, but he drove them a little way from the site and they walked through something called Stonehenge Avenue. He told her that this was the ceremonial route to the ancient site and that they were walking in the footsteps of their Neolithic ancestors. He spread his waterproof coat out for them to sit beneath a row of beech trees. And, as the sun rose over Salisbury Plain, Charlotte was left speechless by the breathtaking spectacle of the summer solstice taking place below them. It was beyond words.

As she peered through the drizzle now, Charlotte couldn't help but reflect the difference in her feelings then and now. She couldn't imagine Ed doing anything that spontaneous these days. Everything he did was planned and plotted down to the minutest detail. She sighed. What on earth had happened to them?

Her thoughts were interrupted by Sam's groan from the back seat. 'Mum, this is so boring! Who cares about a load of old ruins? It's raining and it's my turn to sit in the front!'

'You're right,' she said, peering out gloomily through the windscreen at the procession of tourists trudging around the fence. Resignedly, she waited for the children to swap seats. 'Pass me a sandwich from that M&S bag.' She took a bite, started the car and pointed it towards Cornwall.

*

They arrived in Pendruggan three hours later. Apart from a false alarm when Alex had shouted that Molly was hanging her head in that funny way she did before she got carsick and they had to make an emergency stop, the journey was uneventful. Alex was in a world of her own, plugged into her headphones, while Sam kept up a constant prattle on the subject of Spike Turner and Casper flips and pop shove-its and nosegrinds. Charlotte was pretty good at tuning him out when she needed to, though she couldn't help feeling that Sam deserved a more receptive audience – and, if his father could only be bothered to be a more available dad, he'd have one.

They all cheered when the sea finally came into view. By this time the weather had brightened considerably and Charlotte was heartened by the sight of the sparkling blue expanse. She loved the sea, and it always had the power to make her feel good. Everything was better by the sea, wasn't it?

As they entered Pendruggan, she was thrilled to see that it was a typical Cornish village with rows of robust cottages rendered in local stone, their doors painted in bright seaside colours. Some of them had lifebuoys and upturned lobster pots and nets lying in their front gardens. Charlotte wound down the window so they could hear the loud cries of the gulls that circled above.

In the centre of the village was a green, and around it she could see that all the needs of the villagers could be met: there was a shop, a church with what looked like a beautiful vicarage close by; there was even a red telephone box that actually seemed to have a working phone inside it.

Her satnav directed her to a turning that led to a row of cottages. She drove carefully up the gravel track.

'Look at that cute one, Mum.' Alex pointed at an extremely pretty cottage called Gull's Cry. They drove to the end and Charlotte felt her heart lurch when she saw Ed standing outside what must be their holiday let. It had been over four weeks since they had last set eyes on each other – the longest they'd ever been apart. Even when he'd been filming abroad, they'd always managed to slot some family time into the schedule, with Ed flying home or the rest of them flying out to visit him on location.

She pulled up in front of the cottage; there was no driveway, just a small front garden filled to bursting with lavender, rosemary, hebe and other scented shrubs. Alex was the first out of the car and she threw herself at her father, who hugged her back tightly.

Sam was close behind, chattering excitedly as his father rubbed his hair and slung an arm around his shoulders. Determined not to be left out, Molly bounced around Ed's legs, yapping excitedly.

Ed waved to Charlotte, waiting for her to join them before ushering the children inside. She was aware that she was taking an age to park the car. Her insides tightened again and she took a deep breath to steady herself, knowing that this flutter of nerves was a precursor to the conversation that she and her husband needed to have.

*

'What do you think?' asked Ed, eager for her approval. It seemed to him that the cottage was every bit as perfect as Penny had said it would be. The front door opened straight into a small but perfectly formed living room with a wood burner in the fireplace. It was snug and cosy, with comfy sofas and cushions strewn around, though it had probably taken a lot of hard work on the part of the owners to make it look so casually thrown together. Through the back was a kitchen that had everything a family on holiday could need, and dotted around everywhere were pictures of boats and the sea.

'It's amazing, Ed,' Charlotte agreed, and Ed felt himself breathe a sigh of relief. He'd been on tenterhooks for hours, wondering what she'd make of it.

They trailed after the children as they raced up the stairs to check out the bedrooms, with Molly bringing up the rear. There was a double with an en-suite and two single bedrooms, plus a bathroom.

'This one's mine!' joked Sam about the master bedroom.

'You'll be lucky.' Ed ruffled his son's hair.

The children bickered good-naturedly over their rooms as Charlotte checked out the en-suite bathroom.

She ran her finger along the side of the antique Victorian bath. 'They've thought of everything, haven't they?' she said, clearly impressed.

'The owners have only recently put it on the rental market and it's getting towards the end of the season, otherwise we wouldn't have got a look-in.' Ed sat down on the edge of the bath and pulled his wife towards him. 'I think this is big enough for two, don't you?'

Charlotte gave a little shake of her head, but held his gaze. 'Looks small to me.' Then she deftly slipped away from his embrace and headed back out to the hallway, entreating the children not to let Molly jump on the bed.

Ed's heart sank. The look in his wife's eyes was guarded, distant, but he cautioned himself not to rush things. It was always like this after a big job away; they needed to find their way to each other again; get the first row out of the way and the first night in bed together – whichever came first, hopefully the latter – then get back to normal. *Be patient . . . Give her some space*, said the voice in his head.

Putting on a bright smile, he went to join the others, who were now admiring the view from Sam's designated bedroom.

'What do you think that is?' Sam was pointing to a shedlike structure in a large garden beyond.

'Penny said it belonged to someone called Tony. Apparently it's a shepherd's hut.'

'Is he a shepherd, then? I can't see any sheep.'

Ed tried to recall what Penny had told him about the man who lived there, but it eluded him for the moment. 'I'm sure they must be around somewhere,' he said vaguely. 'Anyway, the tour's not over yet – and the best is yet to come!' He couldn't keep the bubble of excitement out of his voice; this was the part he had been looking forward to most.

Charlotte eyed him curiously. 'Oh?'

'Come on.' He slipped his arm around Charlotte's waist and ushered her to the stairs. 'We're going for a little walk and you are going to love what we find at the end of it . . .'

*

It was by now late afternoon and the sun was starting to sink towards the horizon. As Ed set off with his family in tow, heading past the church and down a path that led to the sea, they could hear the sound of the waves getting closer, and the unmistakable smell of the sea filled their senses.

As they rounded the headland, Ed heard Charlotte gasp as she took in the view.

'Oh, Ed, it's beautiful!'

'It's called Shellsand Bay.'

Below them a gentle path led down the side of the cliffs to the most beautiful beach. The late sun cast its rays on the clear blue water set against a cloudless azure Cornish sky. Ed had been desperate for the weather to be perfect for their arrival; he wanted everything to be just right. Knowing how much Charlotte loved the sea, he turned to see whether Shellsand had had the desired effect. Even after fifteen years together, the sight of her took his breath away. Her green eyes looked bluer with the sky reflected in them, and the gentle breeze ruffled her fair hair.

'I love it,' she said simply, drinking in the colours and the rolling cliffs as they tumbled towards the golden sands.

'I thought you would.' He smiled as he took her hand. 'But there's more to come. Follow me.'

At the bottom of the path, as the beach opened up in front of them, Ed pointed towards a small row of beach huts. 'Look.'

There were about half a dozen of them, all painted in primary colours. One or two looked as though they could use some love and attention, with faded paint and rusty hinges, but

Ed led them to a bright-red hut that had obviously been well cared for. A Cornish flag fluttered from the roof. There was a step up to a small veranda outside the padlocked entrance. Ed took the step, brandishing the key. 'It's ours!'

Alex shrieked, her teenage 'whatever' face momentarily forgotten. 'Seriously, Dad, this is awesome!'

'Come on, Dad, let's have a look inside,' Sam urged, leaping onto the veranda.

Ed put the key in the padlock and had to wriggle it around for a moment before it turned.

'Hurry up!' urged Sam, jumping up and down with impatience.

'Keep your hair on!' Ed turned the handle and at last the door creaked open.

The interior of the cabin was more spacious than it looked from the outside.

'Cool. It's like the TARDIS in here,' observed Sam.

There was an old fifties kitchen dresser in the corner. Charlotte opened the doors: it was full of mismatched crockery. There was a tin tea caddy filled with teabags and little pots containing sugar, instant coffee and lots of other useful things. A kettle sat on one of the shelves and there was a sixties Formica-topped table with two chairs. In the corner, propped up against the wall, were deckchairs, a windbreak, a barbecue and all sorts of other beach paraphernalia. Sam was beside himself when he found a surfboard and a trunk containing wetsuits and snorkels.

'Dad, we've got to try these!'

Ed wasn't so sure. 'They look a tad snug,' he said cautiously. 'They might not fit . . .'

'Dad, they're made of rubber – they'll stretch. Besides, you're thin as a stick insect.' Sam made a stretchy-rubber face.

'Well, let's think about it, shall we?' Ed had never been surfing and didn't consider himself to be very athletic. Hopefully, Sam would be distracted by something else before he was called upon to deliver on that front.

'What do you think of it, Charlotte?'

Charlotte, who was lovingly fingering the bleached wood on the veranda and gazing out at the rolling surf, turned to him, her eyes shining joyfully. 'I don't know what to say. I never expected anything like this.'

Ed stood beside her and put his arm around her shoulder, gently pulling her towards him. She didn't resist, and a moment later her arm found its way around his waist. He'd forgotten how good she felt.

'It's an amazing place, Ed. I can't believe you've never brought us here before.'

'This is the first time we've ever had a break in the schedule. Usually I'm so busy the whole time I'm down here, I don't venture far off the set. I never really thought of it as a holiday place.'

Ed felt Charlotte's hand drop away from him. He looked down at her face. She gazed out steadily towards the horizon, but said nothing.

'What are you thinking?'

She was silent for a moment and he held his breath, waiting. 'Nothing.' She turned to him and smiled, her smile reaching her eyes for the first time since she'd arrived. 'Nothing. I'm so happy to be here, Ed. It's perfect.'

And Ed found himself hoping that this would turn out to be true.

3

Ed was so disorientated when he awoke that it took him a moment to remember where he was. He fumbled for his glasses at the side of the bed, then set about looking for his watch. His mother had given it to him after his father died; despite a few scratches and knocks, it had served him well. It wasn't a particularly expensive watch – just a stainless-steel Accurist with a mesh strap – but Ed thought it was quite cool in a seventies sort of way. It kept his dad close, though he'd been dead now for over twenty years; cut down in his prime by cancer.

He was stunned to see it was 9.30. How had he managed to sleep in so late? Even when he was at home, he was normally an early riser, so attuned to the hours of a filming schedule that he didn't need an alarm clock. He must have been more tired than he realised.

It took a moment for it to sink in that the bed beside him was empty.

The previous evening, they'd driven to the nearest town, Trevay. It was a typical Cornish seaside resort and the queue outside the Fairy Codmother fish-and-chip shop snaked down the seafront. They sat on the harbour wall with their food on their laps, the children happily chucking chips to the aggressively hovering seagulls while Molly looked on incredulously as she was denied even one – Charlotte was always pretty strict about not rewarding dogs who begged. Ed waited until she wasn't looking before giving Molly his leftovers, then they returned to the cottage and he opened a bottle of wine. He'd sipped from a glass while trying unsuccessfully to light the wood burner, while behind him Alex and Sam argued about what movie to watch on Netflix.

'You decide, Charlotte,' Ed suggested. '*The Wedding Singer* or *Ghostbusters?*'

'*Ghostbusters*, obviously.'

'Mum!' Alex protested. 'We've seen it a million times already.'

'Don't drag me into it, then. I'm going to hit the hay anyway.'

'You're not going to stay and watch?' Ed was disappointed, he was hoping that they could have a cuddle on the sofa – get closer again – but Charlotte insisted she was too exhausted after the long drive.

'I can hardly keep my eyes open. Don't let the kids stay up too late. Night, you two.'

Ed watched her as she kissed the tops of the children's heads, then made her way up the stairs. Just before the bedroom door closed, her voice drifted down: 'Don't drink all of that bottle to yourself or you won't be able to sleep.'

The kids drifted off to their rooms before the end of the film and, by the time he had tidied up and made it to bed himself, Charlotte was in a deep slumber, curled up in a foetus position on the far side of the bed. *She might as well be on the far side of the world,* he thought glumly as he climbed under the covers, wishing the gulf between them would disappear.

Now, he swung his legs over the bed and padded across to the en-suite bathroom. On the way, he caught sight of his naked torso in the large mirror that hung over the dresser. He stopped for moment to study his reflection; he'd never had to worry about putting weight on. He seemed to have hollow legs – 'nervous energy', Charlotte called it – but he thought he could see a creeping tyre around his middle. He jabbed at it, trying to remember when he'd last exercised. A few years ago he'd taken up running as a way of getting rid of some of that excess energy so that he could get a good night's sleep, but over recent months he'd felt so drained and lacking in motivation that he'd abandoned his daily run. Perhaps that was why he was sleeping so badly.

He slipped on his jogging bottoms and yesterday's T-shirt and headed downstairs. The staircase was narrow and the wooden steps felt cold beneath his feet.

He was surprised to see Sam already awake and engrossed in his iPad. 'Morning, Sam. Where is everyone?' He plonked himself down on the sofa next to his son.

'Mum's taken Molly for a walk and Alex's still in bed.'

'What you looking at?'

'Spike Turner.'

'Who's Spike Turner?'

Sam rolled his eyes and tutted. 'Dad! He's the world number-one skate pro and, like, the most awesome dude, like, ever.'

'Right. I see.' Though he didn't. 'What's he doing?'

'Honestly, Dad, do I have to explain everything?' Sam pointed to the screen. 'Watch this!'

Ed watched as a man of about thirty five in a baseball cap, baggy jeans and a Superdry T-shirt skated towards a flight of steps, launched himself on his skateboard and coasted down the handrail, before flipping his board 360 degrees, executing a perfect backflip and then landing on his board.

'Wow!' Ed had to admit it was pretty impressive. 'But isn't it about time he got a proper job – at his age?'

'Skateboarding *is* a proper job, Dad. He's a multimillionaire!' Sam looked at him with wide eyes. 'That's what I'm going to do when I grow up.'

'How many skateboard millionaires are there?'

'Loads!'

'Mmm.'

'Dad, Pendruggan looks too lame to have a board park, but I saw some dudes with boards when we were driving back from that fish-and-chip shop. Can we go and find it? Please, Dad?'

'Maybe later. You hungry?'

'Do bears shit in the woods?'

'Sam, mind your language, mate.'

'Sorry.'

'The full works?'

'Yes!' Sam and his dad fist-bumped and Ed headed over to the open-plan kitchen. He hoped that Charlotte had picked up some supplies yesterday, though he hadn't noticed what was in the large selection of bags and holdalls when he'd unpacked her ancient Volvo. He opened the fridge door – it was a huge American-style one – and was pleased to see breakfast ingredients: eggs, bacon, sausages, mushrooms, plus a few peppers and onions, some milk, cheese and a loaf of bread. There was even fresh coffee in the cupboard. He smiled, relieved that he wouldn't have to tramp into the village before his caffeine fix.

He set about clattering around the kitchen, pulling out saucepans, frying pans and chopping boards. Breakfast was well on the way by the time Alex came downstairs. Her hair was scraped back in her trademark ponytail and she was rubbing sleep from her eyes.

'God, Dad, are you trying to wake the dead?'

'Good morning, my treasure!' He kissed her on the top of her head. 'I like your jimjams.' He pointed with his wooden spoon at her Hello Kitty pyjamas.

She threw him a sarcastic look. 'They're ironic.'

'Of course they are, my little princess.'

Alex playfully gave him a push and then sat down next to her brother.

'Oh, no, not Spike Turner again.'

'Feck off.'

'Sam, enough with the potty mouth,' Ed warned.

'*Feck* isn't a swearword, Dad.'

'Don't push your luck.'

The first proper bicker of the day was nipped in the bud by Molly's arrival as she bounded joyfully through the front door, followed by Charlotte.

'It's a glorious day out there. Oh, good – breakfast. What are we having?'

'Don't interfere – you know this is my speciality.'

'I wouldn't dream of it.' She leaned in and gave Ed a peck on the cheek. 'Though you do seem to have used every single pot, pan and utensil in the entire kitchen.'

'It's a man thing. We need our man tools.'

'It's an organisation thing – or lack of it – if you ask me.'

'I didn't. Sam, Alex, I'm dishing up. Can you lay the table?'

There was then a chaotic scrum as the small kitchen was filled with three bodies all rummaging around in drawers and cupboards that they weren't familiar with, while Charlotte sat down at the table with the paper.

'That village shop's quite something. There's a funny woman in there, some ancient Cockney.'

'Ah, that's Queenie, what she doesn't know isn't worth knowing. Right – here it comes.' He set loaded plates in front of Charlotte and Sam, who fell on them eagerly. Then he went back for a pile of buttered toast. 'Yours is coming, don't worry,' he told Alex.

A moment later he was back with a plate for himself and one for his daughter. He was halfway through a Waitrose Cumberland sausage when he realised that Alex was still staring at her untouched plate.

'What's wrong?' he asked.

Charlotte looked up from her paper. 'Oh.'

'Oh, what?'

Everyone was looking from their plate to Ed. 'What?'

'Dad, Alex is a vegetarian,' Sam said through a mouthful of scrambled eggs.

'Since when?' Ed was flabbergasted. 'The last time we ate out, you had that giant burger, remember? With two burgers, bacon and blue cheese – it was fifteen quid,' he added, still aghast at the bill.

Alex pursed her lips and put her head to one side, speaking to him in a patronising voice: 'I've been meat-free for over a year now, Dad.'

'Yes, that was probably the last time we went out for a meal,' Charlotte said matter-of-factly. 'And I can't remember the last time you sat down to a meal at home without jumping up to take a phone call or check your email every five minutes. You probably didn't notice.'

'But you used to love my fry-ups.' Ed was aware that a whine had entered his voice.

'I still do, Dad, but not with any of this.' And she used her fork to push one of the sausages towards her father.

Ed was struck speechless. How had he managed to miss something so obvious?

Charlotte reached out for her daughter's plate. 'Want me to make you something else, darling?'

Determined to retrieve the situation, Ed leapt from his chair. 'Hang on – give me a chance – what do you want instead? Poached eggs on toast? Welsh rarebit – have we got any cheese?'

'An omelette – a nice one and not too runny.'

'Right,' said Ed. 'The perfect omelette on its way.'

'Can I have Alex's bacon and sausage, then?' Sam was already moving his fork towards Alex's abandoned plate.

Charlotte laughed. 'Here – go nuts. I'll put your dad's breakfast in the oven to keep warm.'

A few minutes of banging and clattering ensued as Ed cleaned the frying pan and prepared the ingredients. The delicious smell of sautéed mushrooms and onions wafted over, until eventually Ed presented his daughter with a golden omelette, butter still bubbling away on the surface. 'Well?' he asked anxiously. 'Is it perfect?'

Alex put a forkful into her mouth and gave it a delicate chew. 'Pretty much.'

Ed breathed out. 'That'll do.'

Charlotte waved for him to sit down, then retrieved his half-full plate from the warm oven before rolling her sleeves up to tackle the huge pile of washing-up.

When he'd finished eating, Ed joined his wife at the sink, whispering, 'So did I pull victory from the jaws of defeat?'

'Just about,' she answered, not looking up from her task. 'This time. But there's no such thing as perfection. Not in families and not in omelettes, either. It takes practice to even be half good, let alone perfect.'

'What do you mean?' Ed could tell there was a subtext to what she was saying, but he couldn't get a handle on it.

'I mean . . .' She put down the pan she was scouring and looked up at him. 'You might be able to manufacture perfection on a three-day holiday, but it's much harder for me to do it every day at home in Worthing. On my own.' She turned away to dry her hands on a tea towel, then tossed him a scouring pad. 'Seeing as you're demonstrating how to be the perfect husband and father this weekend, how about doing the rest of the washing-up?'

Deciding that the best policy was to say nothing, Ed took the scouring pad and finished washing the dishes.

*

After breakfast, keen to make the most of the late-summer sunshine, they set off for the beach cabin. As they made their way down the path, they could see that, while the beach wasn't as busy as some of the sandy beaches in the area, Shellsand Bay had its own unique charm. With no direct road leading to the beach, it could be reached only from the path, which made access difficult for buggies and wheelchairs, and limited the number of casual visitors. But the Atlantic swell guaranteed excellent waves, making it a surfer's paradise, and it also had a devoted following among those who appreciated its natural beauty and sheltered position in the lee of the cliffs.

Charlotte had packed everything they needed for the day into their cooler bag and an assortment of beach bags. Although the sun was shining, there was a chill in the air, so she hadn't taken any chances, bringing along blankets, towels and cardigans in case the weather took a turn for the worse.

Once in the cabin, Ed pulled out the deck-chairs and the windbreaker, fashioning a little area in front of the veranda. The clapboard doors of the other beach huts were all padlocked, so they had that part of the beach to themselves.

Charlotte stuck the kettle on, pulling out some green teabags from one of the carriers. 'Fancy a brew?' she asked Ed.

'Got any coffee?'

'There might be some in the dresser.' She had a rummage in the cupboard and found a jar of Mellow Bird's. It was lumpy, but it would do.

Sam made straight for the surfboard and wetsuits.

'Come on, Dad – let's have a go.'

Ed was reluctant but aware that he'd dragged them all down there and this might be the price he'd have to pay. Tall, at six foot four inches, he'd always felt like he was all clumsy legs, especially when dancing or roller-skating. Now in his forties, he was rarely required to do either, though he suspected that surfing might expose the same sort of awkward gangliness and lack of coordination.

'OK, why not? How do you get one of these things on?' he said with more enthusiasm than he felt.

While Ed and Sam pulled out the squeaky rubbery suits and tried to work out which part went where, Alex plonked herself down on one of the deckchairs and pulled a book from her bag.

Charlotte, meanwhile, was busy exploring. Next to the cupboard was a little, bleached, white wooden table about waist height. There was a gingham curtain around it, and when she pulled it aside she could see a bowl and some washing-up liquid, as well as some tea towels. She'd noticed a standpipe on the beach at the bottom of the path, so that must be where the water came from. Cute. In fact, there were cute things all over the place, from frames filled with old seaside postcards and seaside knick-knacks adorning every surface.

'Now, where are the mugs?' she said to herself.

Opening the bottom of the dresser, she couldn't see any mugs but she did see something else which caught her eye. There were some very old board games, including snakes & ladders and ludo, Scrabble and Yahtzee, as well as a few jigsaw puzzles, but she also spied an old Tea Time biscuit tin. She pulled it out and prised the lid off. It was filled with colour pencils and a few sticks of charcoal. Peering further inside the cupboard, she could also see a supply of artist's paper and a couple of sketchpads. She pulled them out and flicked through the pages; someone had already drawn several pretty pictures of the local area. One of them was of the cabin. It was a little amateur, but the colours and the flag were pretty accurate. Across the top of the picture the artist had written, 'The perfect place to be yourself'.

She smiled and gathered up all the materials – it would be the ideal beach occupation. *And who knows?* she thought. Maybe she would find herself again.

*

Hearing the sound of her husband's laughter, Charlotte looked up from her sketchpad. Despite Ed's protestations, Charlotte could see that he had quite taken to the surfboard. While their thrashing and floundering might not, strictly speaking, be classed as surfing, he and Sam seemed to be having a lot of fun.

In her own quiet way, she too was having fun. For the last couple of hours, she'd been trying to capture the scene in front of her. Drawing by the sea had been a favourite pastime of her childhood, back in the days when her parents would set up the wind-breakers and sun shade and picnic hamper for long summer days on the beach near

Weymouth. It was there that she'd acquired a lifelong fascination for the ever-changing colours of the sea and sky. No sooner had you picked out the subtle teal and turquoise tints of the waves than the clouds would shift and the tones would shift to purple and grey. After a couple of attempts she had decided it was impossible to capture a moment in time; better to be more impressionistic. The figures of Ed and Sam were fluid dashes, as was Molly, the rest of the holidaymakers and surfers mere traces against the cerulean blue of the sky and the cobalt brilliance of the sea.

She put down her pencil and scrutinised her work. Overall, she was pleased with it. She hadn't quite got the shade of the sky right, but she hadn't been aiming for perfection. Her stomach rumbled. Breakfast seemed hours ago.

As if on cue, dripping with sea spray, her son and husband came running towards her.

'Mum, the sea's freezing! Even with the suits on, it's wicked. What's for lunch?'

'You're a bottomless pit, Sam Appleby.' Though only eleven, Sam was already shooting up and looked set to be as tall as his father. 'Sausage sandwiches for you. Cheese for Alex. Egg-mayo for anybody.'

Sam narrowed his eyes. 'Normal egg-mayo?'

'Yes. Normal egg-mayo.'

'You didn't put anything weird in it – not like last time?'

Charlotte feigned shock. 'I don't know what you could possibly mean. Of course there's nothing "weird" in the egg-mayonnaise sandwiches. What a funny boy you are!'

Sam wasn't convinced. 'I'll have sausage. What've you been doing, Mum?'

'Mum's been working on that drawing for ages,' Alex said, putting down her book and springing to her feet. 'Come on, show us.'

Alex and Sam peered over her shoulder at the sketch, Sam dripping seawater on the page.

'Careful!'

'Wow, Mum, that's reeeeally good!' Sam congratulated her.

Charlotte couldn't help preening slightly.

'Well, *I* quite like it.'

Alex feigned indifference. 'Yeah, it's OK. I forgot that you used to be an artist or something.'

'What do you mean, "used to be"?' Charlotte bristled.

'I mean before, when you had a proper job. Wasn't it something to do with art?'

Charlotte instantly made the transition from bristling to prickly. 'For your information, I was a design director on a number of TV programmes and films. Yes, it was something to do with art and, yes, you do need to be quite good at it. As far as I know you don't stop being artistic just because your womb has been commandeered for the purpose of having children. The two aren't mutually exclusive, you know!'

Alex merely shrugged and looked bored, returning to her deckchair and her book.

Charlotte stood, hands on hips, glaring.

'Look, love, I don't think Alex meant anything,' said Ed, trying to smooth her ruffled feathers. 'She wasn't thinking, that's all.'

Still fuming, Charlotte turned her glare on Ed, who attempted what he hoped was a concerned and sympathetic smile. To her it seemed condescending.

'It's an incredible picture,' he gushed, digging himself in deeper. 'And I think it's great that you've found an outlet for your creativity while we're here.'

For a split second, Charlotte felt like strangling him. Instead, she said through gritted teeth, 'Could you try and be a little more patronising, Ed. You're almost there, but you've not quite managed to make me feel completely, utterly belittled – though you're obviously trying very hard.'

Ed's face fell. Charlotte felt a twinge of guilt for turning on him, but it was too late. Her anger was in full flow.

'How do you know that I don't already have an outlet for my creativity, Ed?' she went on, her voice rising an octave or two. 'Though it would actually be quite difficult, wouldn't it, seeing as I'm raising our children practically on my own? I'm not surprised they've forgotten what I'm capable of – all they ever see is the mum who cooks, cleans and nags!'

'Charlotte, I'm sorry, I didn't mean—'

'Oh, forget it. I'm going to take Molly for a walk and stretch my legs.' She grabbed Molly's lead from the rail and Molly shot out from the beach cabin where she'd been keeping out of the sun. 'Come on, Mol, let's go!' she called, striding off in the direction of the cliff path without so much as a backward glance as she added, 'The sandwiches are in the cooler box. Help yourself.'

*

Ed took a bite of egg-mayonnaise sandwich. As the first tang hit his taste buds, he realised that there was something mixed in with the egg and the mayonnaise, something that crunched and that didn't quite work. It tasted odd. He put it back in the sandwich bag.

'Where's Mum gone?' Alex plonked herself down next to him.

'For a walk.'

'Is she in a huff?'

'Possibly.'

'Sorry.' Alex drew a circle in the sand and looked sheepish.

'Never mind. As much my fault as yours, and you know it won't last.'

'Why isn't Mum a . . . design director any more?'

Ed sighed and wondered how to put it.

'Working in film and TV isn't exactly compatible with a normal family life. The hours are crap and production companies don't tend to make allowances for working mothers. The two don't mix.'

'She likes her job at the theatre.'

'How do you know?'

'She's always on the phone to Henry talking about it. He's the director. She spends most of her time at the theatre. Sometimes she asks me to be at home for Sam when he gets back from school because she's running late.'

Ed felt a hot flush rush up his face and tried not to focus on what could be making her late. *I love you . . . can't live without you . . .*

'Will Mum ever go back to work properly? Like before?'

He started to answer but then realised he had no idea whether Charlotte had ambitions in that direction. When the children were little, Charlotte hadn't wanted to leave them, but once they were both at school they had discussed the possibilities. Ed knew that Charlotte missed her work. But jobs were few and far between, and those that did come were either too far away or the hours couldn't fit around the children. Eventually, the subject was quietly dropped. Ed's career had taken off and Charlotte had seemed content to help out at the local theatre, which put on short runs that were geared towards families. 'I don't know, Alex,' he sighed.

'Dad, there's someone waving at you – over there.'

'Where?'

Alex pointed at a woman coming down the path. 'Put your glasses on, Dad!'

Ed scrabbled around in the sand for his specs and put them on. The blur formed itself into Penny coming into view. He smiled widely and waved her over.

'Good God – Alexandra, is that you?' Penny exclaimed when she saw Alex. 'You're just like your father!'

'Hopefully she'll grow out of it. Hello, Pen.' Ed stood and gave her a big hug.

'Hi, Penny.' Alex gave Penny a hug too before joining her brother and Penny waved to Sam who waved his spade back in return.

'How's it going?' she asked. 'This is an

amazing place, isn't it? It has a completely different feel when you're not working.'

'I know. It's perfect. Well . . . almost.'

'Where's Charlotte?'

'Um, she's gone for a walk.'

'Things still a bit rocky?'

'Maybe.'

'Give her time – *your* time. And don't give up.'

He ran his hands through his hair. 'I'm trying.'

'Isn't that Charlotte coming down the path?'

Ed turned and saw his wife heading towards them with Molly. The tense bad humour was gone from her face, but there was a definite flicker of caution in her eyes when she registered Penny Leighton's presence – effectively her husband's boss.

'Hi, Pen, lovely to see you!' Charlotte gave Penny a hug. They knew each other well.

'Have you been walking on the cliffs? Majestic, aren't they?'

'Yes, and the perfect antidote to disappearing up my own arse.' Charlotte shot Ed a quick glance. 'Not trying to drag my husband away from his holiday, are you, Pen?'

She said this lightly, but Ed knew there'd be trouble if he reneged on his promise.

'Not on your nelly! Simon's banned me from talking about work, so no worries on that score.'

'How's your lovely daughter, Jenna?'

'Exhausting! But we've got a night off this evening. Why don't you all come and join us for dinner at the Dolphin later? Don and Dorrie are doing a hog roast and all the locals will be there.'

Charlotte looked at Ed, uncertain.

'No work talk, we promise – don't we, Pen?'

'Brownie's honour.'

It took Charlotte a nanosecond to make up her mind. 'You're on!' She gave Penny a huge grin. 'I could do with a pint of Cornish Knocker!'

*

The Dolphin was packed out. Holidaymakers and locals alike seemed to be making the most of summer's last hurrah. Ed, Charlotte and the kids made their way through the throng and found that Penny and her husband,

Simon, the local vicar, had saved them a seat at a table with two of their friends: Helen Merrifield and Piran Ambrose.

They all shook hands and said their hellos, then Piran, Simon and Ed duly trooped to the bar, as men do, while the women got chatting about life and kids.

Charlotte warmed to Helen immediately. It came as a surprise that Helen was now a grandmother – Charlotte thought she was way too young. And she seemed so at home in the community that it was hard to believe she'd left her husband and moved down here from London only recently.

'I thought Piran was your husband.'

'Good God, no!' Helen laughed. 'We'd end up killing each other. I've been there, done that, and he's way too grouchy to be a full-time boyfriend. I know you've got to take the rough with the smooth, but he takes the biscuit sometimes, so it's better this way.'

It turned out that Helen lived a few doors down from their holiday let, in Gull's Cry – the cottage she'd admired when she arrived.

Helen clapped her hands. 'Fabulous, I can

take you for a tour round the village. I'll introduce you to Queenie and Tony.'

'Oh, yes, I've already met Queenie.'

The men rejoined them at the table. 'Guess what: Piran's a proper Cornish fisherman!' announced Ed. He had a boyish flush, and Charlotte suspected he was already a bit pissed, but she was glad to see that he was enjoying himself.

Piran gave them a stern look. 'Proper fisherman are the only kind we have in this part of the world. 'Tis a serious business.'

'Yes, of course. I'm not much of a fisherman myself. I only went once with my dad, and neither of us could bear to kill the poor buggers. We threw most of them back in.'

'I could never, ever kill a fish. They have the same feelings as people and catching them is murder!' Alex said with feeling, looking up from her iPad.

A smile danced around Piran's lips. 'Aye, maid, their lives is as precious to them as yours is to you. All good fisherman respect that and only take what they need.'

'Ha, that's funny, Alex,' continued Ed, getting into his stride. 'I seem to remember that you ended up killing quite a lot of fish when you were younger. Your fish tank had what you might call a revolving-door policy!'

'That wasn't the same thing, Dad!' she protested, but she laughed along with everyone else.

'At least it can't be as bad as Mum,' Sam chipped in. 'She's been prosecuted for crimes against fish dinners! Harry Potter wants her prawn surprise recipe so he can use it to defeat Voldemort!'

'You don't appreciate fine dining, that's your problem,' protested Charlotte, but she was laughing too.

The laughter was interrupted by Alex's ringtone, which was an incredibly loud and annoying jangle.

She looked at the caller and answered it quickly, whispering into the phone that she'd call back when she was alone.

'Got a secret admirer, Alex?' Ed joked. 'Make sure you don't bring him home on prawn-surprise night – that might be the last we see of him!'

Alex's face went puce and she balled her fists.

'Ed, hang on . . .' Charlotte could see immediately that Alex was upset. But Alex had already stood up and was facing her father, blushing hotly.

'You don't know what you're talking about. You don't understand and you don't even care!' Then she stomped off to sit outside on the terrace.

'What did I say?' Ed looked aghast, stung by the ferocity of her words.

'Teenagers – they're a mystery,' said Simon, with a sympathetic shake of his head.

'It's getting late. Perhaps we should go.' Charlotte started gathering up their things, casting anxious glances out to the terrace, where Alex could be seen furiously texting on her phone.

They all said their goodnights, Helen and Charlotte promising to see each other again. Charlotte retrieved Alex from the beer garden and the two of them walked on ahead with Sam and Molly, while Ed followed gloomily behind.

'She seemed so angry,' he said to Charlotte hours later as they lay in bed. Outside the night air was still, punctuated occasionally by a barn owl emitting its blood-curdling scream as it swooped on its prey. 'I've never seen her like that before.'

'She's very touchy.' Charlotte said sleepily from her side of the bed.

'But it's so unlike Alex. She hates confrontation, even if she *is* a sulky teenager.'

Charlotte sighed from the depths of her pillow, then propped herself up on her elbows and turned to face Ed. 'She's been like this for a while now. Something's bothering her, but she won't confide in me. If you'd been around more, you might have noticed before now.'

There was no vitriol or accusation in her words – it was a merely bald statement. They both knew the truth of it and there was nothing Ed could say in his defence.

He ran a hand over his face. 'I know, I know – it's just been so hard to get home. Maybe I can reschedule a few things, put a few projects on the back burner . . .'

'Ed.' Charlotte lifted her hand to still his words. 'This isn't about "rescheduling a few things". Alex is growing up. In a few years she'll be an adult. That's something no one can reschedule. And, if you don't adjust your priorities, you're going to miss what's left of her childhood. Sam's, too. Before you know it, they'll have drifted away from you and you'll never be able to get back what you've lost.' Her voice softened as she saw the impact her words were having. 'Right now, Alex needs us – even if she doesn't realise it.'

Then Charlotte turned her back on him and settled herself down to sleep. As her breathing deepened and she drifted off, Ed noticed a tightness grip his jaw and recognised the familiar feel of a long sleepless night ahead of him.

4

Typically for an English summer, a day of sunshine and blue skies was followed by a gloomy, overcast morning with ominous grey clouds threatening rain. The weather seemed to affect the mood in the cottage and, despite Ed's entreaties, Alex was refusing his offer of a vegetarian fry-up.

'I only want toast, Dad.'

Alex was huddled up beneath the duvet in her bedroom, wrapped in her hoodie. Ed thought she looked much younger than her fifteen years.

'Come on, kitten,' he coaxed. 'A bite to eat and then we can take a trip somewhere. There's a lot to see around here. How about driving to Tintagel? There's a castle.'

'I don't want to tramp round a boring castle.'

'It's not boring – they say King Arthur was born there.'

'Who?'

There'd been a time when Ed could shake his daughter out of a moody spell in minutes. Alex had been a naturally sunny child who was easily reduced to helpless giggles. He realised with a pang of disappointment that those days were gone. Getting a laugh today would be like getting blood out of a stone.

'Brown or white?'

'Brown. White bread is full of additives.'

'So virtuous – aren't you supposed to be living on McDonald's and alcopops at your age?'

Ed's attempt at playful banter merely drew a roll of the eyes before Alex pulled the duvet over her head, signalling an end to the conversation. Defeated, he headed back downstairs.

Charlotte was putting on her waterproof and Sam was in his usual spot on the sofa, watching an episode of *The Big Bang Theory*.

'Off somewhere?' he asked his wife.

'I'm going to take a walk down to the beach hut with Molly.'

'But it looks like rain. I was going to make breakfast.'

'Not for me.'

'Oh. What about you, Sam? Not going to reject the only meal I'm any good at, are you?'

'Nah, I'm starving. Is it ready now?'

Ed looked in the fridge. Their supplies had been somewhat depleted since yesterday. 'We'll need to go on a foraging expedition. We're running low.'

'Try that shop I was telling you about in the village,' suggested Charlotte.

'Huh?'

'Ed, you'll have me doubting that you hang on my every word if you say things like that. I nipped in there for a paper yesterday morning – you can't miss it: the windows are lined with yellow cellophane and crammed with old boxes of Black Magic and York Fruits. It's as if the last fifty years never happened. The owner's an old Cockney—'

'Oh, you mean Queenie's shop. She does lovely pasties – or "oggys" as they call them round here. You have to order them in advance though. The crew practically live off them when we're filming.'

'Well, I think you'll find she sells groceries and everything else we need to top up our dwindling supplies. I can't believe you've been coming here year after year and you don't even know where to buy a loaf and a pint of milk.'

'OK, Queenie's it is, then. Fancy a trip out, Sam?'

'Aw, I'm watching this!'

'You can watch that any time. Queenie's has to be seen to be believed.'

Leaving Ed to take on the parental duty of tearing his son away from the TV, Charlotte clipped Molly's lead onto her collar and opened the door. It was starting to rain, but she didn't care. The beach cabin was calling her.

*

By the time Charlotte got down the path to the beach, a steady drizzle had set in. Nothing too heavy, but enough to keep most people away. Aside from the odd dog-walker passing by, she had the beach all to herself.

She had left some dog towels in the cabin the day before and the first thing she did after undoing the padlock was to fish them out and give Molly a good rubdown. Molly looked out from behind the long hair that covered her eyes and groaned.

'Don't moan – I get enough of that from the kids! I know you hate the rain, but everything will end up smelling of wet dog if I don't dry you off.'

Molly licked her face by way of apology and, once that was done, she settled down on her dog blanket while Charlotte put the kettle on.

Looking out at the turbulent greys and greens of the surf, whipped up by the rain, Charlotte thought she liked the beach even more today. There was something wonderfully liberating about being here alone. She'd had to get used to being by herself, with Ed away from home so much, but this was a different type of alone. Solitude rather than loneliness. She liked it. The thought of having this on your doorstep every day was hugely appealing and she could see why Helen had come to Pendruggan and stayed put. Maybe when the kids were older . . .

She dismissed the thought. No good daydreaming about something that could never happen – not the way things were.

Taking her sketchpad and pencils from the

cupboard, she settled herself down on a deck-chair on the veranda, well out of the rain. Then she began to draw.

*

Charlotte had completely lost track of time when a voice broke her concentration. On looking up she was surprised and delighted to see Helen Merrifield, accompanied by a lively Jack Russell terrier who danced around her feet. Helen hailed her and headed over. Charlotte waved back, laid her drawing down by the deckchair and put the kettle on. She had no idea how long she'd been there but the weather had brightened.

'Good afternoon, Charlotte. How are you today?'

'Afternoon? What time is it?'

Helen looked at her watch. 'Coming up to one o'clock.'

'Crikey! I've been here for hours. Cuppa?'

'Yes, please, I'm parched.'

Helen pulled out another deckchair and plonked herself down on it, watching as her Jack Russell greeted Molly, the pair of them nose to nose, tails wagging, and then sniffing each other's bum in a doggy hello.

'What's your dog's name?' asked Charlotte.

'Jack – and he's not mine, he belongs to Piran, in as much as he belongs to anyone. He's a law unto himself, that dog. He seems to have taken a fancy to yours.'

Jack was chasing Molly in circles around the beach. Despite the difference in size, Jack seemed to have the upper hand.

Charlotte laughed. 'Poor Molly, she's like a giddy schoolgirl. Has Jack been neutered?'

Helen snorted. 'No dog of Piran's would have his knackers tampered with. Molly?'

'No idea. Don't think so . . .'

'Oh, well, a marriage made in heaven. The mind boggles. Is that your drawing?' Helen picked up the sketchpad from her feet. The picture was a brooding mass of greys and greens, depicting the turbulent surf of earlier. The colours were vivid and dramatic and the picture perfectly caught the atmosphere of Shellsand Bay. 'You're very good, Charlotte. Is this the sort of thing you do at the theatre you were telling me about?'

'Not quite.' Charlotte joined her, handing

over a mug of steaming English breakfast tea. It wasn't a green-tea sort of day. 'The sets are bigger, so you can't be so precise. It's more about getting the right feel for a production and creating a canvas that helps the performers tell the story. You have to think a bit differently.'

'Do you enjoy it?'

Charlotte thought for a moment, looking out to the horizon. 'Yes, I do. It's not the same as working on TV sets, not as exhilarating, but you get to be creative. You have to work very closely with the director, channelling his vision . . .' she trailed off and Helen could sense something beneath.

'I can imagine. It's a collaboration.'

'Yes, Henry's been very . . .' – Charlotte searched for the right word – 'supportive.'

Helen didn't pry further. 'How's the holiday?'

'Oh, not too bad. The usual bickering, but it's always like that, isn't it?'

'Tell me about it!' Helen said with feeling. 'I've lost count of the family holidays that have been marred by squabbles and mood swings and tantrums. They can be quite a trial. All too often it's a relief to go home.'

Charlotte shook her head. 'It's nowhere near

as bad as that. It makes a nice change for us to be together. And this is absolutely wonderful.' She threw her hand out expansively at Shellsand Bay. 'It's just . . .'

'You don't need to tell me,' Helen said sympathetically. 'It's hard for everyone to rub along sometimes, isn't it? Families change and grow, and not always at the same rate. I had a husband who spent most of our holidays chatting up the barmaid or trying to cadge telephone numbers from young waitresses. One day I woke up and realised that, while I'd changed and matured, my silly husband Gray was still the same insecure man-child he'd been twenty-odd years ago. It was liberating to realise I wasn't going to put up with it any more.'

Charlotte nodded. 'Yes, we do change. I can't even remember what I was like when Ed and I first met. I must have been quite confident, but I think it was more bravado than anything. Ed was so intense, took everything so seriously.' She watched a small boat chugging far out at sea, tossed gently by the waves. 'He still does take it all so seriously. I know he seems like a lovely easygoing guy, but he's a worrier, forever driving himself, like he's on a treadmill he can't get off of.'

Helen sipped at her tea. 'Maybe you should swap roles for a while.'

'He'd never be able to do that.'

'Try him. You never know.'

Charlotte frowned, thinking.

'Why not suggest that you both give it a trial run?' said Helen. 'He should embrace change and so should you. If your marriage is solid, then it'll be good for both of you – sometimes a marriage needs a helping hand to get it over that midlife hump. None of us stay the same all our lives, we grow and we change – it's human nature.'

'Maybe.' Charlotte didn't look convinced. Was their marriage solid? 'Are you going back up to the village now? I'll come with you.'

They packed up and Charlotte put Molly on the lead. Jack didn't have one.

'Got time for that village tour? We can pop in and say hello to Polly, who lives next door to me.'

'Why not?'

'By the way, Piran's offered to take you all out on his boat – the weather looks like it's going in the right direction, so how about this afternoon?'

'What a great idea! Thanks, Helen.'

'It's no problem. I'll text Piran.'

'Not just for that . . . I mean, you know . . . the tea and sympathy.'

'Any time.'

The two women exchanged a hug and headed back towards Pendruggan.

*

Charlotte loved Polly's cottage. It was full of wind chimes and the scent of jasmine. Polly gave her some Tregothan tea – 'It's good for your chakras' – and she fed Molly an organic vegetarian dog treat, which Molly ate politely though with a certain lack of enthusiasm.

There was a bounce in Charlotte's step when she got back to the cottage to find Ed and Sam on the sofa watching surf videos on YouTube.

'We went to Queenie's,' Ed told her. 'I'm afraid she didn't have any oggys left for our lunch, but I got some stuff for sandwiches.'

'Mum, come and have a look at this,' Sam

said. 'We've been watching these huge waves and—'

'Put that thing away. The sun's shining and we're going out for the afternoon.'

She skipped up the stairs to find Alex still in her room. 'Hey. How's it going?'

Alex grunted something incomprehensible from beneath her hoodie.

'Sun's out.'

'I don't like the sun.'

Charlotte laughed. 'Or anything else for that matter, it seems. Stop hibernating, let's go out.'

'I'm tired. I don't want to tramp round a stately home or a lobster farm.'

'Ah – I've got something much better than that in mind.'

Alex's interest was piqued. 'Like what?'

'Fancy a trip out on a fishing boat?'

Alex sat up – she loved boats. 'Piran's?'

'Who else's!'

'Awesome! When are we going?'

'Now?'

Alex jumped out of bed and Charlotte headed back downstairs to rally the troops.

*

An hour later they headed out of Trevay on Piran's fishing boat. The rain had cleared and the sun kept breaking through the clouds, promising warmer weather to come. The family foursome were all decked out in lifejackets and chatting excitedly as the boat chugged out into the open sea.

'Backalong times, Trevay was full of little boats and fishermen like me,' Piran informed them. 'Nowadays, it's the big boys like Behenna and Clovelly Fisheries what gets the big catches, but some of us still stick to the old ways.'

They spent the next few hours learning about tackle and lines. Despite his gruff manner, Piran was a patient and thoughtful teacher. Alex and Ed were in their element. Alex had always been fascinated by how things work, and Piran's informed explanation of long-line fishing and how to set the lines near the surface kept her completely absorbed.

Sam and Charlotte were more interested in watching the wildlife. They thought they saw a dolphin's fin and definitely spotted a couple of seals popping their heads out of the water, eyeing them curiously.

'I've caught some!' Alex was thrilled when

she felt the tug of mackerel on her line. Neither Ed nor Charlotte wanted to spoil the mood by reminding her of her vegetarian principles.

After a happy afternoon, they headed back towards Trevay. To everyone's delight, a pod of dolphins appeared alongside the boat and raced them for a few minutes before breaking off and disappearing back under the waves. Charlotte watched in awe as the lithe creatures darted beneath the water. She remembered that the ancient Celts believed that dolphins had healing powers. Was it too much to hope that this could be the start of the healing process for her family too?

*

When they pulled into the harbour and unloaded their catch, everyone agreed that a barbie down on the beach would be the perfect end to a perfect day. Charlotte filled a cooler box with ingredients that Ed had picked up from Queenie's shop, along with their fish.

Aside from a fry-up, Ed's other speciality was a barbecue. He loved the rigmarole of setting the charcoal – never briquettes – getting the glow just right, and then judging with minute precision whether it was time to put the food on. No charred-on-the-outside-raw-on-the-inside frozen sausages on *his* watch.

As Ed set the barbecue going in the fading evening sunlight, Sam tackled Alex about her mackerel, half a dozen of which hung from a string attached to a hook outside the cabin.

'If you're a vegetarian, how come you've gone fishing?'

Charlotte held her breath for a moment, fearing that the blue touchpaper had been lit and an explosion would surely follow.

But, after taking a moment to consider her response, Alex said calmly, 'Fishing felt different than I thought it would. Piran explained that fishing didn't have to be destructive as long as you fish responsibly and think about your impact on the environment. I liked setting the lines and doing it properly.'

'Are you going to eat one?'

'I'm not sure.'

'Well, I'm hoping they'll be delicious,' Ed chipped in. 'But I wish we'd asked Piran to gut them as well.'

'He'd have told you not to be a "bleddy lazy

up-country arse" and to do it yourself.' Charlotte came alongside him, carrying a chopping board and a plastic bowl filled with new potatoes and some beetroot, which she placed on the camping table. 'What are you going to cook them in?'

'I've got a marinade of lime, ginger and chilli.'

'Nice! I'm starving.' She handed him an open beer and took a swig from her own.

'Cheers.' They chinked bottles.

As the cooking got under way, the appetising smell from the fish was unbearably tempting and Alex found herself hovering by her dad as he dished hot fish onto plates.

'Want some?' he offered non-judgementally.

'Go on then.' She picked hot chunks of mackerel off with her fingers and declared them delicious.

'Does this mean you're not a vegetarian now?' Sam badgered.

'I'm a fishetarian!'

There were plenty of other people down at the beach that evening and they stayed on until quite late. Charlotte was disappointed to see that her potato, beetroot and egg salad remained untouched. She was sure that was the list of ingredients that Lorraine Pascale had used . . . But maybe the egg was wrong – or was it the beetroot? She offered it to Molly, who gave her a courteous thank-you lick but left the bowl untouched.

When they got home, Charlotte tidied away the things while Ed collapsed on the sofa and the children drifted off upstairs to bed.

Charlotte poured herself a glass of red wine and one for Ed, but by the time she sat down, squeezed onto the sofa in the tiny space left by his big long legs, he was fast asleep and snoring loudly.

Noticing that his glasses had fallen halfway off his face, she removed them. He never carried a spare pair and would be lost if they got broken. Looking at him now, she thought that, apart from the grey hair around his temples, he looked almost exactly the same as he had when they'd first met. Essentially, he was the same, she realised. Constant. Steady. Just never there these days . . . She wondered what he would say about her.

Charlotte took a blanket and gently tucked it around him, then turned and headed to bed with Molly close behind her.

5

It was the Applebys' last day in Pendruggan. Tomorrow Charlotte and the kids would be going home, and Charlotte was surprised how sad she felt at the idea. She'd fallen in love with the place. As she looked around her at the dozens of families, surfers and walkers who had come to Shellsand Beach to enjoy the late-August sunshine, she thought there was no better place to be than here.

Their imminent departure meant the time for prevaricating was over. Charlotte would have to talk to Ed today. She'd decided what she was going to say and how she was going to say it – she'd have to pick her moment.

For the first time since they'd been on Shellsand Bay, there was a sign of life from one of the other cabins. The one next door to theirs was occupied. It looked to Charlotte like a family of surfers. There was an older man – a well-preserved specimen, perhaps in his late forties – accompanied by a young man who looked to be just out of his teens, and another lad about the same age as Alex. The younger two had blond hair, while the older one had probably been blond once but his hair was now white, with thick Boris Becker eyebrows that stood out in stark contrast against his tanned skin. All three had the sort of tan that comes from year-round exposure to the Cornish elements rather than a few weeks on the beach in summer.

The man was immediately friendly and introduced himself in a thick Cornish burr as Paul Tallack. 'We'm from up Trevay way, but my boys love the waves. Older one's Ryan and my youngest is Josh over there.'

He and Ed shook hands. 'This is Charlotte, my wife, and those are my kids, Alex and Sam.' He pointed to his son and daughter, down at the water's edge. 'You're surfing too?'

'Aye, love it. We all do. Shellsand's got the right climate, see? Today's going be perfect. Them waves is building.'

'How can you tell?'

Paul tapped his nose conspiratorially, then laughed. 'You gotta be in the know. Seriously, I'm a reserve coastguard, so I've spent years watching the waves and learning. You can never second-guess the sea, though. That's part of the wonder of it. Never know what you're gonna get. Need to respect it too, mind – can't take any chances.'

Spotting the presence of real-life surfers, Sam came hurrying up the beach to watch Ryan expertly setting out their kit. Charlotte could see that her husband and son were bonding with the neighbours in that way men do. Perhaps Sam and Ed were going to get that surfing lesson they so desperately needed after all.

Josh, the younger of the two sons, ambled over to where Alex was sitting, still with her head in a book, trying hard to be nonchalant. At about fifteen or sixteen he was already a handsome young man and had that character-istic and confident Cornish charm.

'What you'm reading?'

'Pardon?' Charlotte looked up from her book.

'Your book. What is it?'

'Umm,' Alex looked down awkwardly at the cover, as if she'd forgotten. 'It's called *The Catcher in the Rye*.' She looked down at her book again, her cheeks suddenly bright pink.

Watching from the veranda, Charlotte felt a pang at Alex's awkwardness, but Josh didn't seem to notice. 'What's it about?' He sat down next to her as if it was the most natural thing in the world.

Alex hesitated, looking around her as if to find somewhere to bolt to. But there was no escape. She caught her mother's eye and Charlotte looked away quickly, desperate not to add to her daughter's shyness.

'Er, it's about a boy – he doesn't feel that the world understands him. Or that he doesn't understand the world. He sort of goes off on his own . . .' She trailed off awkwardly.

'Yeah, folks are like that. My dad's all right, leaves me alone, but my mum's always on at us: "Do this, don't do that, pick your trainers up." She don't stop . . .'

Josh continued in this lively vein and Charlotte smiled. Alex didn't stand a chance.

*

The sun was high in the sky. Paul and Ryan couldn't have been happier to share their expertise, and in Ed and Sam they had two ultra-willing pupils. Josh seemed content to forgo surfing and sit with Alex. The two of them were now side by side on the deckchairs, chatting animatedly. Alex's face was lit up in a way Charlotte had almost forgotten, it was so long since she'd seen her that happy. Josh obviously had the knack of breaking down her barriers – his charm offensive was working wonders where Charlotte's and Ed's had failed. Maybe she'd been worrying too much.

When lunchtime arrived, Paul and Ed decided to pool resources on the barbecue front. Was it possible for two men to share barbecue duties? Charlotte wondered. Or would it end in a tongs-off? They seemed to be doing all right, though she almost wished they weren't. Having steeled herself for a difficult conversation with Ed, she was anxious to get it over with. But first they needed a moment alone. A little voice kept niggling away at her: *If you don't tell him now* . . . Her thoughts were interrupted by Paul's voice booming across the beach: 'C'mon, Josh – muck in, mate! Get back to the jeep and bring me some more o' that charcoal, it's in the boot.'

Josh did as he was asked and Alex came over to sit with her mother on the veranda.

'You've caught the sun.' Charlotte observed. 'Given up on the vampire look, then?'

'Mum!' But Alex was smiling.

They were joined by Sam, who proceeded to strip off his wetsuit, scattering big drops of seawater over both of them.

'Watch out, you flippin' idiot!' Alex scolded.

'Don't call me an idiot. At least I'm not sitting there with an idiotic look on my face mooning over some stupid boy.'

'Shuttup, you little arsehole!'

'Sam,' said Charlotte sharply, 'stop showing off. Alex, calm down and don't let him wind you up.'

But Sam was in that irksome mode that comes as second nature to eleven-year-old boys, and, having discovered Alex's raw spot, he wasn't about to stop poking it.

'Oohhh, feeling sensitive about your new boyfriend?' He puckered up his lips and made loud kissing noises. 'Mwah-mwah, I love you, Joshy.'

'I'm going to kill you if you don't shut up, you little shit!'

'Sam, that's enough!' Charlotte could see that Sam was pushing it too far, but there was no letup.

'Alex and Joshy, sitting in a tree,' he sang, 'K-I-S-S-I-N-G!'

At this Alex launched herself at Sam, shoving him to the ground and kicking him in the ribs, screaming. 'I hate you! I wish you were dead! I hate you and I hate Josh – I hate all boys!'

Despite thinking that Sam had gone too far, Charlotte was shocked at Alex's reaction.

Ed, hearing the fracas, rushed over and hauled the children apart. 'What the hell's going on, you two?'

'That cow pushed me over and kicked me!'

Sam was rubbing his ribs and feigning tears, but Alex was panting hard and real tears of anger were streaming down her face.

Ed took her by the shoulders. 'Alex, relax. Come on, let's chill for a minute, OK?'

'No, it's not OK.' Alex shook her head violently. 'Don't tell me to chill out. Leave me alone.' She shrugged her father off and moved away.

'Alex, please, talk to me—'

'No. Leave me alone, all of you. I'm going to take Molly for a walk.' And, before he could stop her, Alex grabbed Molly, who'd been tethered to the veranda to stop her going near the barbecue, and stormed off in the direction of the path.

'Ed? I'm not sure we should let her go off like this . . .'

'Let's give her some space, Charlotte.'

'I don't know – she seems really upset.'

'She just needs a bit of time to calm down, that's all. As for you . . .' Ed turned to Sam and launched into a serious telling off.

Charlotte caught snatches of it drifting on the breeze – *no iPad* and *apologise to your sister* – but her thoughts were with Alex as she watched her climb the path up the cliffs.

*

Over forty minutes had gone by and Alex still hadn't returned. The food had been dished up but neither Charlotte nor Ed could muster an appetite. Even Josh was asking after her now.

'I'm going to go and look for her,' announced Charlotte.

'No, I'll go.'

Their conversation was interrupted as the insistent beep of a pager came from Paul's pocket. He took it out, looked at it and then made a call on his mobile.

'OK, mate. I'm on my way.' He rang off. Gone was his carefree, happy-go-lucky demeanour. He turned back to them with a look of tense concern. 'There's no need to panic yet, but a fishing boat on the water close to here has reported a sighting of a body down on the rocks.'

Charlotte's hand flew to her mouth. 'Oh, my God! Alex!'

'Now hang on a minute,' said Paul, laying a reassuring hand on her arm. 'There's no reason to assume that it's Alex. The best thing you can do is stay here in case she comes back. I'm on callout and we've been scrambled. We'll let you know if there's any news.'

As Paul set off at a run up the cliff path in the direction of his jeep, Charlotte and Ed looked at each other. 'I'm going to find her, Ed.' Charlotte's tone brooked no argument.

'I'm coming with you.' Ed was equally determined. Sam's bottom lip trembled and Ed squeezed his son's shoulder. 'Stay with Ryan and Josh, Sam. Everything's going to be OK, I promise.'

*

Keen ramblers could walk all the way from Pendruggan to Trevay, but Charlotte had never been that far. On her walks with Molly they had only pottered along a short section where slopes dotted with gorse and heather rolled gently down to the sea. Now she found herself on a stretch of the coast path with brambles on one side and vertiginous cliffs on the other. She could hardly bear to look down to where the waves battered the rocks a couple of hundred feet below.

'I'll never forgive myself if anything's happened to her . . .' Charlotte's voice caught as she hurried along the path with Ed on her heels. 'I should never have let her go – I could see how upset she was.'

'Try not to think the worst. We don't know that anything's happened – she might be back at the cottage, playing with her iPad.' But Ed wasn't sure that he believed his own words. Alex might be fifteen, but she wasn't worldly wise and she'd been upset and angry – the possibilities didn't bear thinking about.

They'd been walking for twenty minutes now and there was still no sign of her. Ed had tried calling her mobile, but there was no signal. Charlotte could feel panic rising up inside her with each step. Striding out in front, she picked up her pace. *Please, please, let her be all right*, she prayed.

Then she saw a familiar outline ahead. Alex!

'Darling! Alex! We're here!' Charlotte ran as fast as she dared to where Alex was crouched down, almost at the edge of the cliff. On hearing her mother's voice, Alex stood and threw herself at her mother. The pair of them were immediately enveloped by Ed's strong arms, and for a moment they stood hugging each other and crying.

'M-m-m—' Alex was distraught, tears choking her words. Charlotte held her tightly, whispering soothing words. 'It's all right, baby, it's all right, we're here.'

'M-M-Molly—' Alex could only point down to the rocks below.

'You two, get back from the edge.' Ed took a step forward and peered down the face of the cliff. The drop here wasn't so sharp and the cliff sloped down a little more gently, but down at the bottom of the rocks he could see the unmistakable hairy body of Molly. She didn't appear to be moving.

Despite a surge of relief that it was his dog and not his daughter lying down there, he felt a lump in his throat at the sight below. Behind him, Charlotte was asking, 'Do you know how it happened, Alex?'

Between convulsive sobs, Alex replied, 'We were walking . . . she wasn't on the lead and then she saw a rabbit . . . and then she was gone . . .'

'OK, baby, OK.'

'I didn't want to leave her, Dad. I tried to call for help, but I couldn't get a signal . . . At first she was barking, and I was telling her it was going to be all right, but I couldn't see any way to get down to her . . . And now she's not moving.' Alex broke into fresh tears.

'The main thing is to get you to safety.

Charlotte, can you and Alex make it back to the beach? I'll wait here for the coastguard.'

'OK.' Charlotte gave her husband a brief but fierce hug and he kissed them both on their heads.

As they headed back up the path, Ed dropped to his knees and looked down at Molly's prone body.

'Hang on in there, girl,' he whispered as the outline of the coastguard's red rescue vessel rounded the headland.

*

'You must be the owners of the luckiest dog in Cornwall.' Paul's face was one huge grin as he jumped out of his jeep and led Molly to the door of the cottage.

The four family members threw themselves at their beloved pooch. Molly couldn't believe the overwhelming but welcome attention she was receiving.

'We pulled up in the boat and she jumped up straightaway, barking like a good 'un – think she must have been asleep.'

'Well, that's one way of dealing with a crisis!'

Charlotte regarded her dog with admiration while Molly gazed back at her dopily from beneath her fringe, her fluffy tail wagging furiously.

Alex hugged Molly more tightly than anyone else and buried her face in the dog's mane. 'Molly, you big hairy twit.'

'You all right?' asked Josh, coming up the path behind his father.

Alex stood up and waved for him to join her. The two of them went to sit on the low dry stone wall that enclosed the front garden, their heads close together, engrossed in conversation.

'She'll be fine.'

'We can't thank you enough for everything you've done.' Ed took Paul's hand and clasped it gratefully in thanks.

'Just another day for the coastguard, no 'arm done and all's ended well. I've earned me pint tonight, that's for sure.'

'We owe you more than a pint,' Charlotte said with feeling.

'I'll hold you to that!' Paul winked at her, then returned to his jeep, waiting patiently in the driver's seat while Josh and Alex swapped numbers. Then Josh jumped in and they drove off.

'I hope we see them again,' said Alex, joining her mother on the sofa.

Charlotte put an arm around her daughter. 'I'm sure we will, darling. We all want to come back here, even Molly does.' Molly wagged her tail at the sound of her name.

Alex's face was buried in her hoodie and Charlotte could feel her shoulders shaking as more tears came. They'd all had a big fright today, so she wasn't surprised that Alex was still feeling fragile.

'I'm sorry I called you a shit and pushed you over,' Alex told Sam.

'What?' Sam looked up from his iPad, where he'd been engrossed in his new obsession – Surf World. 'Oh, that? Don't sweat it.'

Alex smiled through her tears. 'You are annoying, though.'

Ed squeezed in next to his wife and daughter on the sofa. He gave Sam the head nod that said *Hop it*. Sam rolled his eyes at his dad's unsubtle hint, but for once restrained himself from making a clever remark.

'Come on, Molly – let's go bark at that cat

that keeps hanging around for scraps outside.' He bounded out of the back door, followed by the luckiest dog in Cornwall.

Alex continued to hold on to her mum, and Charlotte was reminded of when Alex was a baby, hating to be put down or held by anyone else. Those days were long ago, but it seemed her little girl still needed her mum after all.

'What is it, darling? Is there something else upsetting you?'

Alex didn't say anything but the question brought on a torrent of tears. Ed came and joined them on the sofa.

'You can tell me and your mum anything,' he said encouragingly.

'Not anything!'

'Of course you can!' Charlotte squeezed her daughter's hand. 'Is it something or someone at school? Is it about your new friend – Lily? She's not being horrid, is she?

At this there was a fresh bout of sobbing. 'No, Lily's amazing, I . . . I . . .' Alex hesitated and her parents held their breath. 'I . . . I've got feelings for her . . . I think I might be gay!'

Charlotte and Ed exchanged a brief wide-eyed

look, then immediately rushed to reassure her with shushes, hugs and soothing words.

'We love you no matter who you have feelings for,' Charlotte said forcefully. 'Don't we, Ed?'

'Absolutely! You mean the world to us and as long as you're happy, that's good enough for us.'

'Really?'

'Really, really,' they both said in unison.

Alex sniffed and wiped her nose on her cuff. 'It's just that Josh . . . today . . . he was so nice. We exchanged numbers.'

'Darling girl,' said Charlotte, holding Alex to her tightly, 'you're still working things out. You don't have to be anything yet. Growing up isn't easy and you'll take a few different turns along the way, but you'll sort it out eventually.'

'You don't need to rush anything,' agreed Ed.

'You remember Gloria – my best friend from university?' said Charlotte.

Alex nodded. 'The one with those annoying twins: Gina and Angelina.'

'And two annoying ex-husbands!' Charlotte laughed. 'Well, when we were students, she was head of the Student Lesbian and Gay

Alliance. She had a very handsome girlfriend called Mogs and they were inseparable.'

Alex raised her eyebrows in astonishment.

'You can ask her next time you see her – Gloria's proud of her past. The thing is, people change – it's natural. If you care about someone, all you want is for them to be happy. Nothing else matters.'

*

After a Chinese takeaway from Trevay, Alex had gone upstairs and Charlotte had tucked her in as if she were a little girl again. Then she came down and joined Ed on the sofa with a bottle of red wine.

'What a day!' Ed exhaled loudly. 'Do you think she's gay?'

Charlotte thought about it for a moment. 'Not sure. Maybe. Maybe not. Does it bother you?'

'Nope.'

'Good.'

They sipped their drinks in silence for a while. Then:

'Charlotte . . .'

'Ed . . .'

They spoke at the same time and an awkwardness descended over them.

Not again, Ed thought anxiously.

'There's something I need to tell you . . .' There was something ominous in her tone.

'It's about Henry, isn't it?'

Charlotte looked confused. 'Well, yes – how did you know?'

All Ed's anxieties came bursting to the surface. 'I just do,' he blurted. 'And I know what you're going to say – I saw the texts.'

Charlotte was frowning. 'What texts?'

'The ones that said, "I love you . . .", "I can't live without you".'

He watched realisation dawn on her face, steeling himself for the bombshell to drop, for her to tell him that it was all over between them, that she was leaving. Instead she did the last thing he'd expected: she burst out laughing.

Lost for words, Ed looked at her aghast. How could she find anything amusing in this?

'Oh, Ed!' She tried to compose herself but couldn't stop the hilarity from bubbling over. 'Your face is a picture!'

'Charlotte, I don't understand, what—'

She touched his face tenderly. 'No, you don't understand, do you? After all your years in the business, I'd have thought you understood loveydom! Henry didn't mean me, he meant this.' She took her phone from her pocket, scrolled through her gallery until she came to a series of photographs, and held it out for Ed to see.

Ed found himself looking at the most extraordinary theatre set – and it was clearly Charlotte's design, he'd recognise her style anywhere. 'What is it?'

'The set of *The Lion, the Witch and the Wardrobe*. It's Henry's production and my set.'

Ed knew his wife was supremely talented, but the innovative way that Charlotte had created an ice forest and integrated the vast wardrobe was extraordinary. He scrolled down: there was Badger's cosy underground set, the White Witch's palace, the stone table and Cair Paravel – it was breathtaking.

'I can't believe you've done all this.' Though really he could.

'The production's been a huge success.' She paused and took a deep breath. 'Such a success that it's transferring to the West End. Henry wants me on board – he's asked me to go with him.'

Ed didn't know what to say. Once again, he'd been struck dumb by Charlotte coming out with a momentous announcement that was going to change their lives.

He looked at his wife's face and saw in it the same girl who'd told him she was pregnant all those years ago. The woman who had given up everything for him and for their family.

A brief look of anguish crossed her face, but then it was gone and she set her lips in a thin line. 'Of course, I know I can't go – Alex and Sam need one of us at home, and your job is too important to jeopardise. It was stupid for me to even consider it.' She placed her glass on the table and made to stand up, as if the conversation was over. Ed pulled her back down and held her face in his hands. He was determined that this time he was going to get it right.

'Charlotte Appleby, my beautiful, talented wife. You've given me more than I could ever have expected and you've done the most amazing job of raising our children. I'd be a big wet puddle of worry and stress without you to keep me steady. I would literally go to the ends of the earth if you asked me to. So, if this is what you want, then we're going to make it happen.'

Charlotte looked at him, incredulous. 'Do you mean that?'

'Yes. I mean it more than anything I've said in my whole life. You've done your bit and now it's my turn. I'll tell Pen that she can promote Cassie. I can supervise from afar when necessary and do consultancy work, when I'm not too busy being a househusband, that is.'

'You mean you'll do all the cooking?'

'Yes. I doubt I can manage a prawn surprise, but I think the world will thank me for that, don't you?'

'Hey!' She gave him a playful punch. 'And all the cleaning?'

'I'll even wear a pinny.'

'Why do I find that image strangely erotic?'

'Because you're a bit kinky?'

'I thought you'd forgotten.'

'Impossible.' And, before he could say anything else, Charlotte straddled her husband and started to remove his clothes.

EPILOGUE

Charlotte shook her children gently awake as the sun appeared below the horizon.

'We're here.'

There was much moaning and groaning from the back.

'Mum, why are we doing this again? We already did it on the way.' Sam stretched his arms and let out a huge yawn.

'I know, but this time we've got hot chocolate.' She poured each of them half a beakerful from a brightly coloured Thermos. They all sipped at their cups for a few moments.

'Ready?' Ed asked as he collected up their cups.

'No, it's freezing!'

'Then bring your blankets!'

He opened the door of the Volvo and the

four of them headed along Stonehenge Avenue to the row of beech trees.

They sat down on a waterproof picnic blanket and settled themselves in. Molly gambolled around the field ahead, chasing the flocks of early-morning starlings as they started up their dawn chorus.

The rosy-coloured fingers of dawn crept above the horizon and the sun rose quickly into the morning sky, its golden rays illuminating the ancient triptychs of Stonehenge below them. They watched in silence.

'What do you think?' Charlotte asked the children, drinking in the sight. 'This is the best time to see it. Are you more impressed this time?'

'Maybe,' said Alex.

'I still think it's a bit small,' Sam said, then added quickly, 'But it's pretty cool, I suppose.'

Ed looked at his wife ruefully. 'Kids are always difficult to please – there's no such thing as perfection.'

'No.' But Charlotte wanted this moment to last for ever. The four of them, here together. Her family. 'Except perhaps right here, right now.' She leaned in to kiss her husband.

'Urgh! Get a room!' Sam and Alex shrieked, then ran away across the field, chasing after Molly, scattering the starlings as the sun rose over Salisbury Plain.

The Stolen
WEEKEND

1

'What on earth?' Penny Leighton grappled at the side of her bed, trying to locate her mobile phone as it rang loudly somewhere close by. She blinked, bleary-eyed, at the blue fascia of her iPhone 5 as it flashed insistently at her in the darkness of the bedroom. The usually jaunty, old-fashioned ringtone was the last thing she wanted to hear at six in the morning. This morning in particular. *Who the hell was ringing her at this ungodly hour?*

Penny sat bolt upright in bed as she saw the caller's name appear.

'*Audrey bloody Tipton*!!' Penny angrily pressed the silent button and shoved the vibrating phone back under her pillow.

'What is that woman pestering me for now?' Penny turned over in the bed, directing the question to where her husband Simon ought to be, but was surprised to see that his side of the bed was empty. The Right Reverend Simon Canter, vicar of Pendruggan, was normally an early riser, as members of the clergy tended to be, but she hadn't anticipated that he would have got up at this unearthly hour. After all, it was a Tuesday, no early services today, and last night they'd both got to bed late. Penny was the sole owner of Penny Leighton Productions, a successful TV production company that had a string of prime-time successes under its belt. Her latest hit was a TV show called *Mr Tibbs*, based on the mystery stories of Mavis Carew. The series was filmed in and around Pendruggan, a small, unspoilt Cornish village that Penny had discovered when her best friend Helen Merrifield decided to make a fresh start there after divorcing her philandering husband. Penny had come for a visit and ended up finding not only the perfect location for *Mr Tibbs* but the man she wanted to spend the rest of her life with. Though she would never have imagined herself as a vicar's wife, she'd never been happier. Her loving and gentle husband, with his chocolate-brown eyes and soft-spoken voice, had brought out the best in Penny and she had no regrets about upping sticks to move to Cornwall. Or at least, not until this morning.

Knowing that Simon was up and about, Penny found it impossible to settle back to sleep. She swung her legs out of the bed and reached for her satin dressing gown, which was hanging on a peg nearby. Then she went to the window and pulled open the heavy curtains, which kept out even the most persistent sunshine.

It was April and the sky was still tinged with the night, but the purple and pink fingertips of dawn were already starting to snake their way across the horizon.

'Mmm. Red sky in the morning,' Penny observed. 'Looks like bad weather. Again.'

She trudged down the stairs to find that the house was in total darkness, except for Simon's study, where a gentle light emanated from under the doorway.

Penny knocked softly and popped her head around the door.

'Morning, Vicar.'

Simon's head was buried in what appeared

to be the parish appointments diary. Penny could tell from the way his fingertips were pressed against his furrowed brow that he was feeling harassed.

'Oh, good morning, darling.' He looked up from his desk, blinking at her through his glasses. 'Sorry, did I wake you?'

'I'm not sure it is quite morning yet,' Penny replied. 'And no, it wasn't you who woke me, it was a phone call from that busybody, Audrey Tipton.'

'Really, what did she want?'

'Dunno – I cut her off.' Penny looked down at her iPhone. 'But it looks as though she left me a message.'

'You should be having a lie-in. You look done in.'

'I feel done in. The last few weeks have been really gruelling. I'm so exhausted, I couldn't even enjoy the wrap party.'

'I'm sorry you had to go alone, darling, but there was so much to do here,' he sighed guiltily.

Penny walked over to her husband and gave his balding head a kiss. 'Oh, stuff that. You didn't miss anything: it was only the usual shenanigans. The lead actors all lording it over each other and getting pissed while the runners and researchers snogged one another.' She peered at the papers spread over his desk. 'What's the problem? Is there anything I can do to help?'

Simon put down his pen, took off his glasses and ran a hand anxiously over his shining scalp. 'It's this whole business with the new vicar at St Peter's.'

The church of St Peter's was in Trevay, the nearest town and a thriving seaside resort. It had been without its own vicar for months and Simon had been asked by the bishop to help out with services until a suitable candidate was found to fill the post. As if it wasn't enough having two congregations to minister to, Simon was also expected to supervise the builders carrying out restorations to St Peter's bell tower. As a result, the last few weeks had been as gruelling for him as they had for Penny. They'd barely had a moment to themselves and were both exhausted.

'The verger at St Peter's Church has been taken ill,' Simon told her. 'He's been a godsend, helping me out with the services and keeping things ticking over. Without him, I just don't know how I'm going to cope. We've got two funerals scheduled tomorrow morning – one here and one in Trevay – at the same time, so I'm going to have to phone around and find someone to officiate.' He looked up at her despairingly. 'And it doesn't end there. Until the verger recovers, I'll have to cut evensong down here so that I can dash over to Trevay to take the six p.m. service, and then there's—'

Penny laid a gentle hand on his shoulder. 'Have you told the bishop? Surely he can sort something out?'

'I called the diocese secretary yesterday, but the bishop is on a retreat until next week. I probably won't see him until he shows up to bless the new bell tower. There's so much to organise, but I already feel as if I've been pulled in half – there's only so much of me to go round.' Simon's pinched face was etched with worry. Penny's heart went out to her beleaguered husband.

'Oh, Simon. Poor you. Have you even had a cup of tea yet?'

He shook his head.

'Well,' said Penny, giving Simon an encouraging smile, 'ecclesiastical matters may not be my forte, but I do know how to boil a kettle.'

*

Later that morning, at a more civilised hour, Penny knelt on the sofa in the cosy sitting room at the vicarage. From this vantage point, she was able to see the last of the trucks loading up the dismantled sets of the *Mr Tibbs* shoot. The set was a painstaking reconstruction of Fifties village life, strategically placed in front of a terrace of Sixties council houses whose occupants were well compensated for the inconvenience. All in all, everyone was happy: the TV crew did their utmost to keep disruption to a minimum; the actors mingled cordially with the residents; locals and visitors alike came to watch the location shoots and the popularity of the series had given tourism in the area a much-needed boost. There was little conflict, but the occasional voice of dissent could sometimes be heard.

It was usually the same voice.

Penny held the phone away from her ear as Audrey gave vent to her feelings.

'The success of your programme owes every-thing to the co-operation of we, the villagers! Without us, *Mr Tibbs* would be a complete failure, Mrs Canter!'

Penny took a deep breath. She'd already been listening to Audrey for ten minutes. Apparently, the woman's neurotic, smelly and aged cocker spaniels had been disturbed by the crew dismantling the set early this morning, hence the dawn phone call.

'Yes, Audrey, we do everything we can to avoid disturbing anyone, but if the crew leave it any later there's a risk the trucks could hold up through traffic at rush hour, or what passes for rush hour in this part of the world.'

It took another ten minutes of yes, Audreys, no Audreys, and three-bags-full, Audreys before Penny was able to get her off the subject and onto another one. But predictably, even then, it was an unwelcome topic.

'So, as vicar's wife, it is incumbent upon you to represent the qualities of charitable benevo-lence, which is why the Old People's Christmas Luncheon Committee have nominated you as chairperson. Our first meeting will be held in the church hall tomorrow at five p.m., we will expect you there.'

'What?!' Penny couldn't believe her ears. 'Who nominated me? I'll have you know that I've given myself two weeks' holiday after a very long and punishing shoot. I've no intention of doing anything other than putting my feet up!'

'The *committee* nominated you.'

'Who's on the committee?'

'Geoffrey and I, of course, and Emma Scott – Pendruggan's Brown Owl. It's a great honour for you. And it's not merely a token role, either. Your task will be to drum up support. The Old People's Christmas Luncheon is a village institution. The old folks rely on it.'

'But it's only April.' Penny said, weakly.

'December will come around sooner than you think. Tomorrow at five p.m., remember.' And with that, Audrey rang off, leaving Penny under a cloud of doom.

*

Helen Merrifield was feeling damp, cold and miserable. Cornwall had just endured its wettest and wildest winter on record, and while

Pendruggan had got off lightly compared to many of the coastal communities, it hadn't emerged completely unscathed. The lovely, cosy charm of Helen's old farmworker's cottage, Gull's Cry, had been severely compromised by the constant deluge of rain. The tiny, slow trickle that had started in one corner of her bathroom had turned into a steady drip-drip, the drips multiplying with each fresh rainfall until the upstairs ceilings were a patchwork of weeping stains and the bedroom floors were littered with pots and pans and buckets.

'Piran! Come and look at this – the one in the bathroom is definitely getting worse!'

Piran Ambrose was Helen's boyfriend and the epitome of brooding masculinity. They'd been together for a while, but they didn't live together. Both valued their independence and knew that sharing a house would drive them nuts. Much of the time Helen found his dark and mercurial nature quite thrilling, but it could also be a blooming pain the arse. This was one of those pain-in-the-arse moments.

His deep Cornish bass reverberated up the stairs. ''Aven't got time. Gotta dash.'

This was immediately followed by the clatter

of buckets being overturned as Helen came dashing out of the bathroom and down the stairs. She managed to catch him before the front door of the cottage had creaked fully open.

'Where are you going? You promised me that someone would come out to have a look at it. That was days ago and we're still waiting.'

'Think you're the only one with a leaky roof? There's plenty worse off than you, maid, and I can't be expected to sit twiddling my thumbs, waiting!'

'So I have to sit around and twiddle mine! But of course, my time isn't important, unlike Piran Ambrose, historian of note!'

Piran frowned at the sarcasm in her voice. 'What exactly have you got to do that is more important than my job?'

'Er . . .' Helen faltered momentarily, but then rallied: 'I promised to run Queenie down to the surgery later. Her bunions are playing up.' She jutted her chin out defiantly.

'Bunions, eh? Really? How taxing for you.' Piran was quite good at sarcasm himself when it suited. 'Look, maid, we're talking about the discovery of a Roman fort here! This is the most significant find Cornwall's seen in decades

– and it's only two miles from my own doorstep. Opportunities like that don't come along
very often in a historian's life. The archeological
team need all the local support they can get. The
bad weather has hampered the dig and they've
got to work quickly if the site isn't going to
be washed away by more bad weather.'

Piran and Helen stood at the door and
looked out at the ominous sky.

'But what about me and the cottage? Aren't
we in danger of being washed away too?' she
asked plaintively.

Piran shook his head and headed off towards
his car, speaking as he went: 'Look, I've asked
Gasping Bob to come out. He should be here
later.'

'Who?' Helen shouted after him.

'Gasping Bob!' And with that, Piran climbed
into his pickup and sped off.

'For some reason,' Helen said to herself, 'that
name doesn't inspire me with confidence.'

*

'Where's my phone?' Simon's panicked voice
carried through the hallway and upstairs to

where Penny was hunting for some ibuprofen in the bathroom cabinet. She was finding it impossible to wind down. Even though the shoot was over, the phone hadn't stopped ringing with requests and queries for Simon. His stress levels were starting to get to her now. She'd slept badly and had a throbbing pain in her shoulder, not to mention the remnants of a hangover.

'By the front door, on the sideboard,' she shouted back, riffling through the packets of aspirin, indigestion remedies and vitamin C tablets.

Moments later, another anxious shout: 'My car keys, where are they? I just had them in my hand.'

'Oh, for heaven's sake!' Penny gave up her fruitless search and headed downstairs. She found Simon anxiously hopping from foot to foot. 'Where did you have them last?'

'Just now!' His voice was a strangled screech.

'Calm down, darling. They won't have gone far.'

Penny's eyes spied his Nokia, still on the sideboard, and next to it a set of keys.

'Here you are, Simon. You must have put

them both down when you put your coat on. Now, is that everything?'

'Er . . . not sure, possibly not. Look, I've got to go – I've should have been at St Peter's ten minutes ago! Bye.'

He planted a distracted peck on her cheek and then dashed out the door.

As the house settled into silence, Penny let out a sigh of relief. 'Right, now for half an hour on the sofa with a hot-water bottle on my shoulder.'

Switching her mobile phone off, Penny boiled a kettle, filled her hot-water bottle with its Paddington Bear cover – tatty and much loved since childhood – and headed off to put her feet up. She'd no sooner arranged herself on the sofa than the doorbell rang. Penny pretended not to hear it. It rang again. More insistently this time.

'Bother, bother, bother.'

Penny launched herself from the sofa and stomped down the corridor. She threw open the door, ready to tell whoever it was to bugger off, but managed to bite back on the words when she found herself confronted by the toothless grin of Queenie Quintrel.

Normally Penny would have been delighted to welcome the ancient Cockney proprietress of the village store, but right now she wasn't it the mood. She offered a tight smile. 'Queenie. What an unexpected pleasure.'

Queenie had run the village store for longer than anyone could remember. An evacuee from London during the war, she'd stayed on and married a local man. She'd never lost her accent, and her outspoken manner and blue rinse were as famous as the home-made pasties she sold in her shop.

'Wotcha, Pen. Ain't you expecting me?' An untipped fag dangled between her lips, its blue smoke wisping its way into the Vicarage.

This left Penny on the back foot. 'Er, should I be?'

'Yeah! You ain't forgot, 'ave yer?'

'Possibly.'

'The Great Pendruggan Bake-Off, ain't it! Raising money for the St Morwenna's Respite Home for the Elderly. We're all supposed to be making something and you and me was gonna be a team, remember?'

Penny's heart sank. Yes, she did remember now. How could this have come around so quickly?

'But I thought that was months away?'

Queenie gave one of her trademark cackles. 'Well, it was months away, months ago! I did tell Simon to remind you I was coming round today when I saw him at church on Sunday.'

'He's got so much on his mind, he must have forgotten. Does it have to be today? You see, I've . . .'

Queenie wasn't taking no for an answer. 'It's gotta be today. I've got Simple Tony in, minding the shop for a couple of hours, but you know what 'e's like! Anyway, the first round of judging is tomorrow and we're on. Dontcha remember, we've called ourselves "The Best of the West". I'm doing the best of Cornwall with my Cornish pasty pie and you're doing the best of London with those little puff-pastry cheesecakes, Richmond Maids of Honour.'

'But I haven't done any shopping . . . the ingredients . . . the recipes . . .?'

'Never you mind about that, dearie. I've got all we need in this little bag of tricks.' Queenie stood aside to reveal a bulging tartan shopping bag on wheels, fit to bursting with bags of flour and other sundry items.

'Now shove out the way. We'd better get a move on.'

Penny stood aside as Queenie wheeled all before her. Her shoulders sagged, as she felt all resistance drain away – along with any hope of five minutes' peace.

2

Helen ended up waiting in all day for 'Gasping Bob'. Despite leaving him numerous messages, there had been no word from Piran. Presumably he'd been so absorbed in his Roman fort that he'd forgotten all about her. That evening, the storm took a nasty turn as another weather front settled in over the region. Helen made her way up to bed with a strong sense of foreboding about what the latest bout of wind and rain would do to her little cottage. She slept fitfully and was already awake when a large chunk of her bedroom ceiling caved in, the water cascading down the flaking plaster and all over her John Lewis symmetric weave, thick-pile rug.

Not normally given to crying, she sat in stunned silence and surveyed the wreckage of what used to be her bedroom. Feeling the hot well of tears threatening to bubble over, Helen realised she had reached some sort of breaking point. Grabbing her dressing gown, she made her way down to the front door and pulled on her wellies. Within minutes she'd jumped into her little car and driven the short distance to Piran's house. It took a few angry thumps on the old wooden front door before his gruff voice could be heard from within.

'All right, keep your ruddy 'air on. Where's the fire?'

The words died in his mouth as he took in the vision of his usually elegant and graceful girlfriend. Sopping wet and looking like she'd been dragged through a hedge backwards, Helen fired out her words like short, sharp pistol shots.

'If I have to suffer one more night of Chinese water torture in my own home, I, Helen Merrifield, am personally going to beat you, Piran Ambrose, to death' – she yanked a sodden and muddy welly from one foot – 'with this Wellington boot!!' She brandished it at him.

For a moment Piran could only stand there in his hastily pulled-on boxers, gawping at her. Then he collapsed into gales of helpless laughter. Helen promptly burst into tears and Piran scooped her up, took her inside and then tucked her up in his bed.

*

It was now Thursday morning and Helen was watching slightly aghast as a man of indeterminate age, but somewhere between eighty-five and one hundred and five years old hoisted a ladder from the top of a battered white van and staggered towards the door of Gull's Cry. His wispy grey hair was tied back in a ponytail and he wore the tightest of skimpy shorts that showcased the knobbliest of brown knees. He was wearing a T-shirt bearing the legend *Cornish Men Do It Slowly* and a brown roll-up poked out of the side of his mouth.

'This is Gasping Bob? The man who's going to fix my roof?' she whispered to Piran, incredulous.

'Don't judge a book by its cover, maid.'

Piran greeted Gasping Bob like a long-lost friend and Helen was surprised to see the old man shoot up the ladder and onto the roof with the agility of a geriatric Tarzan.

Moments later, he'd assessed the damage and was back down again.

'Well, what do you think?' asked Helen.

Gasping Bob shook his head and said, 'Ah . . .'

'Is that good news or bad news?'

He shook his head, shrugged his shoulders and said, 'Ah . . .'

'Well, are you going to fix it?'

'Ah . . .'

Helen turned to Piran. 'Please tell me that this man is going to fix my roof. I don't think I can take much more of this.'

Piran looked at her with irritation. 'Leave the man to do his work and stop wittering, woman.' And with that, he and Gasping Bob wandered off in a huddle and carried on their private conversation in what sounded to Helen like more ahs and umms.

Helen balled her fists in annoyance. 'Bloody Cornwall! Bloody Cornish men!'

And with that she headed off across the village green to the vicarage in hope of finding a cup of tea, or something stronger.

*

'So, you're camping out at Piran's until further notice then?' Penny poured them each a cup of tea from the shiny brown teapot and offered her friend a chocolate HobNob.

'Looks that way, but we'll drive each other nuts after a few days. He can't bear to have a woman cluttering up the place and he's impossible to live with – just so bloody male, and Cornish male to boot.' Helen sipped her tea. 'Got anything stronger?'

'Brandy? Can't join you – Simon's car is playing up again and I'll have to pick him up in Trevay.'

'No fun tippling on your own,' Helen responded. 'What about you – you look exhausted?'

'I am. It's been one thing after another. What with the shoot, then Simon's stress levels, plus the whole village contriving to drive us into an early grave . . . I spent most of yesterday baking with Queenie for this Pendruggan Bake-Off thingummy and then, to top it all, we only went and won the first heat.'

'Congratulations!' Helen registered the thunderous look on Penny's face. 'Aren't you pleased?'

'Pleased? That's the last thing I needed! Now I'll have to go through the whole blooming thing again next week. There's four heats and then a grand final, with Mary Berry herself coming to judge. Still, it'll be a lovely feeling if we beat Audrey Tipton. That woman is the bane of my life.'

'Oh yes, very satisfying.'

'All I want to do is to crawl into bed and shut the world away. The post-production of *Mr Tibbs* will be a walk in the park compared to this lot. Living in Pendruggan can sometimes feel like being beaten to death with a tea cosy!'

The two friends nibbled on their HobNobs glumly.

'Wait a minute! I've had an idea.' There was an excited gleam in Penny's eye. 'I got a call from the director of *Mr Tibbs* today. We're all supposed to be having a break before post-production starts, but he told me there are a few problems with the sound quality and he's getting David Cunningham to come to the dubbing studios to re-do a couple of things.'

Helen nodded, wondering where this was leading.

'David's only free for a few days before he moves on to a new project, so they're recording this weekend,' Penny continued, her voice bubbling with excitement. 'While they don't *need* me, strictly speaking I should be on hand to make sure all goes well. Which gives me the perfect excuse to nip up to London for the weekend. All I'd have to do is literally pop my head in to make sure that everything's tickety-boo – once I've done that, we can have the whole weekend to ourselves. What do you think?'

Helen sat up and clapped her hands together.

'London! Oh, Pen, that would be just the tonic we both need. Cornwall's lovely, but right now, I could just do with a bit of an urban fix. Pizza Express!'

'Yes!' said Penny. 'Twenty-four-hour corner shops that sell everything from corn plasters to condoms!'

'Harvey Nicks, Selfridges, M&S!' Helen said gleefully. 'And I'm sure we could squeeze in dinner at Chez Walter. I've such a craving for their slow-roasted pork belly!'

'I'm a sucker for their venison cottage pie, myself.' Penny grabbed her friend's hand conspiratorially. 'We could even have a night at Mortimer's.'

'Oh, God! Champagne cocktails to die for, in the heart of Mayfair! Let's go now, now, now!'

Suddenly the excitement evaporated from Penny's face and she slumped back in her seat. 'Hang on, what about Simon? He's really under the cosh at the moment. It would be too awful if I left him to it.'

'Oh, come off it, Simon's got loads of help. What about the blue-rinse brigade? They always muck in, don't they? And it's only for a couple of nights. Piran will be glad to get rid of me and my constant nagging.'

'I'm not so sure about Simon. We all agree that I'm not the greatest vicar's wife, but he does rely on me. The trouble is, I've had it up to here with it all.' She waved a hand above her head. 'If I don't get away, I'm afraid our marriage will suffer. Is that terribly selfish of me?'

'Of course it isn't.' Helen gave her friend an encouraging smile. 'You do more for Simon than you realise: you keep him on the straight and narrow; you're his gatekeeper, holding all the busybodies at bay. You've just worked twelve weeks solid, around the clock – you deserve a break.'

'I know,' said Penny, miserably. 'But I'm not sure Simon will agree.'

*

'But the timing is terrible.' Simon's face was full of consternation. He had been in the study, working on his sermons for the coming weekend's services, when Penny had come in to broach the subject of going away. His reaction had been much as she'd expected.

'I know. But they really can't manage without me,' she said guiltily, knowing it was a fib. 'It's my job to be there,' she added, which at least was technically true.

'Well, I'll just have to manage without you then. I'm sure that some of the other villagers will help out here in Pendruggan.'

'Of course they will, darling. They've never let you down.' *Unlike me*, she thought.

'But you will be back here on Tuesday, in time for the blessing of the bell tower?'

'Yes, Simon, I'll make sure we're home by then.'

'*We?*' Simon raised his eyebrows questioningly.

'Oh, Helen and I are travelling together – didn't I mention it?'

'No, you didn't.' Simon's face was suddenly serious. 'I realise that you have your own life, Penny, but being a vicar's wife is important too.'

Penny felt a hot flush of shame creep up her neck, but she needed a break, dammit. Couldn't he see that? It wasn't as if she was running off to join the bloody circus!

'Simon, I promise, I'll be home on Sunday. It's just a quick hop. You'll hardly even notice I've gone.'

She gave him a hug that was returned only reluctantly.

Leaving Simon to his sermons, she closed the study door, tiptoed down the hall and then did a little dance for joy. Despite the pangs of guilt, the prospect of her forthcoming great escape filled her with euphoria.

She sent a text to Helen:

Pack that Mulberry weekend bag. I'm booking us on tonight's sleeper. Bring wine! Px

3

Penny and Helen arrived at Truro station in good time to rendezvous with their overnight-sleeper train to London Paddington.

'What a complete stroke of genius this is!' remarked Helen. 'I've never been on a sleeper before.'

'The last time I went on one was over twenty years ago,' replied Penny as they climbed aboard the waiting train. 'Went to Cornwall for the summer while I was at uni. Got myself a job in a pub in Newquay. Beach all day, worked like a Trojan until the pub shut, then went clubbing every night. Had a ball.'

'Holiday romance?' Helen's eyes twinkled.

'A few.' Penny winked. 'One really hot life-guard called Merlin. He had loads of other girls on the go too, of course, but I didn't care. I just wanted some fun.'

'Fun – that's all we girls want, right?'

'Right!' Penny agreed. 'Especially this weekend. But first we need to find our compartment.'

They wandered up the corridor. 'Ah, here we are!' Penny stopped outside their berth and opened the door. Inside, it was narrow, but there were two decent-sized bunks, one upper and one lower.

'Bagsy I'm having the top one!' said Helen.

'Hey, that's not fair!'

There was an unseemly scuffle as both women laughingly tried to throw their bags onto the top bunk. Through sheer force of will, Helen won out, but justice was delivered when she climbed ungainly up after her bag and promptly banged her head on the ceiling.

'Serves you right,' said Penny, good-naturedly.

'Oh Pen, what an adventure.' From her vantage point, Helen took in the little wash basin with its hot and cold taps. Each bunk had a snug duvet and plump pillows, and they'd each been provided with soap, a towel and a bottle of mineral water. 'It's all so dinky and sweet.'

'Yep, dinky, sweet and a bit of a tight squeeze. There's a buffet lounge with a bar down the corridor. I think we should decamp there for a bit,' said Penny.

'Another brilliant idea.'

Pausing only to grab their handbags, the two friends set off towards the bar.

*

Helen pointed her finger unsteadily at her friend. 'You look pished. Your eyes have shtarted to go.'

'I'm perfectly sober.' Penny waggled her head equally unsteadily. 'You're mishtaken, me ol' mucker. It is you who is pished. I mean pissed.'

The women giggled loudly, and for longer than was strictly necessary, drawing attention from the adjoining table. Seated at it was a serious-looking middle-aged man, who clearly disapproved. He gave a loud tut.

'I'm sorry? Did you say something?' Penny peered at him over the rim of her plastic glass. Two hours ago, they'd bought themselves a sandwich and a teensy bottle of red wine, from which they would each get approximately one small glass each. In front of them on the Formica table now lay the detritus of their half-eaten prawn mayo sandwiches, plus eight teensy wine bottles.

Without a word, the tutting man closed the tablet he was reading and stood to leave.

'Was it something we said?' Helen asked innocently.

The man tutted again but avoided their eyes as he made his way back to his own compartment.

'Men!' said Helen, with feeling. 'Bet he's bloody Cornish too.'

'Don't get us started on Cornwall and Cornish men again! We've worked out that you can't get a Cornish man to do anything in a hurry.'

'They don't like it!' Helen concurred, loudly.

'And,' Penny added, narrowing her eyes, 'they really don't like women taking charge.'

'No, except possibly in the bedroom,' Helen sniggered.

'I'm serious!'

'So am I. You've got to admit it, Pen. Cornish men are very, very sexy.'

'What about Gasping Bob? Was he sexy?'

'Well . . .'

Penny never got to find out what Helen thought of Gasping Bob's sexiness or otherwise because the reply was drowned out by the stewardess pulling down the grille and hanging a closed sign on the bar.

'Sorry, ladies. We're shutting up for the night.' She smiled over at them.

Penny and Helen surveyed the empty bottles in front of them.

'Time for beddywed,' said Penny.

Helen rose to her feet, swaying rather dangerously. Penny did the same and the two women linked arms as they made their way, rather erratically, towards the door. They thanked the stewardess and gave her a wave before making their way out. The exit clearly wasn't wide enough for both of them to leave side-by-side, but they tried it anyway. As Helen collided with the doorframe, she let out another loud snigger.

'Ssssh, people are trying to sleep you know!' came a muffled voice from behind one of the compartments.

'Bet that's Mr Grumpy,' whispered Helen loudly.

Eventually, after much banging and crashing, they made it back to their compartment. Getting undressed and washed was a rather messy affair, but eventually they were both in their cosy nightclothes.

'That's not a onesie you're wearing, is it?' asked Helen.

'Onesies aren't just for kids, you know,' said Penny, peeking out from underneath her rabbit ears, one of which had fallen over her left eye, giving her quite a comical look.

'Simon hasn't seen you like that, has he?'

'Simon loves me no matter what I look like in bed.'

Helen raised a drunken eyebrow. 'I'll take your word for it.'

Too squiffy to care what anyone thought, Penny crawled into her lower bunk, pulling the warm duvet up to her neck.

'Aren't you going to give me a leg up?'

Penny opened one bleary eye and looked up at Helen. 'Eh?'

Helen stuck her bottom lip out. 'I can't get up there. It's like climbing Kilimanjaro.'

Penny thought about it for a moment.

'Pwetty please?' said Helen hopefully, but her

face fell as Penny turned over and was soon snoring like a train.

*

The first thought that occurred to Helen as she emerged from unconsciousness the following morning was that someone had stuck her eyelids together with glue. The second was that the incessant bang, bang, banging wasn't the thudding of her heart or the hammering of her headache, but was in fact, somebody banging loudly on the door of the compartment.

She tried to prop herself up on her elbows but as her eyes gradually opened and took in the scene around her, she saw that next to her head were two feet recognisable as Penny's by the bunny rabbit toes of her onesie.

She gave one of the big toes a hard squeeze.

'Wake up,' she croaked. 'Someone's at the door.'

The only response was a muffled groan from the other end of the cramped bottom berth. Helen slowly got out of the bed, wincing as a shooting pain pierced her temple. Gingerly she picked her way over the untidy piles of clothes and bags and opened the door. Outside was a fresh-faced young steward.

'I'm terribly sorry to disturb you, madam, but we've reached Paddington. I've been banging on the door for ages. I was just about to get the master key to gain access. We thought something might have happened.'

Helen patted her hair in a futile attempt to restore order to what she knew must be her rather dishevelled appearance.

'I'm dreadfully sorry. We seem to have overslept.'

'Heavy night, was it?'

Helen feigned indignation. 'Not in the slightest. The motion of the train must have given us a deeper sleep than usual. That's all.'

The young man looked at her doubtfully. 'People often get carried away on the sleeper, but then they forget what an early arrival we have.'

'Well, we'll just get washed and dressed—'

The young man shook his head. 'There's no time for that, I'm afraid. We've been here ages and you've got to leave by seven a.m. It's already well past that and we can't wait any longer. I'm sorry, but we have to turn the train around or else we'll be in hot water.'

'You mean we have to go *now*?'

''Fraid so.'

'Oh.'

'I'll wait here and help you with your things. There's showers and . . . um . . . facilities on the concourse. You can use them.'

'Er . . .'

But there was no time for arguing. The corridor outside their compartment was bustling with people doing useful things and outside their door a smiling cleaner was waiting expectantly with a J-cloth and a mop in her hands. Once Penny was apprised of the situation, she shuffled out of bed and the two women gathered themselves together as best as they could. There was no time to change out of their nightwear or to arrange themselves and within moments, they were hustled off the train with friendly thank-yous and helpful directions towards the Ladies.

Juggling their coats and bags, Penny and Helen blinked and looked around them. After the cocoon of the train, Paddington station was a hive of activity. All around them, commuters swarmed from trains like ants. The platforms were filled with passengers all coming and going. It was dizzying, and in their present condition they were finding it quite a challenge to orient themselves.

'Where did he say the loos were?' Helen peered uncertainly across the concourse, her hungover brain still confused by all of the activity.

Penny was just about to say that she had spotted the sign for the Ladies when they were approached by a young man with a kindly face. He thrust something into Penny's hand.

'It's not much, but it'll cover the price of a cuppa.' He patted her hand sympathetically before hurrying off down towards the sign for the London Underground.

Penny looked at her palm and saw two shiny pound coins. They looked at each other in astonishment.

'You don't think he thought we were . . .?'

'Bag ladies!!'

'Come on, let's get dressed before we attract any more attention,' Helen said, grabbing Penny's arm and steering her towards the loos.

*

Ignoring more curious stares, they washed and dressed hurriedly and were soon heading towards central London in a black cab.

'Can we please pretend that incident never happened?' said Penny, looking much more respectable in a smart red Burberry mac, though she hid her eyes behind a pair of Dior sunglasses.

Helen feigned nonchalance. 'Pretend what never happened?'

They sped along the Marylebone Road. The route along the Westway was lined with new developments of luxury flats and offices.

'London always seems to be one giant building site,' observed Penny. 'It's forever changing.'

'Unlike Pendruggan, which is always the same,' replied Helen. 'Queenie's had the same display of faded postcards and out-of-date Cornish fudge in her window since the seventies.'

Before long they were driving up Monmouth Street, where the cabbie dropped them outside their boutique hotel, The Hanborough.

'Thank God!' exclaimed Penny. 'Civilisation.'

The hotel was the epitome of luxurious London cool. The foyer was a white oasis of calm; low-slung chaise longues were dotted across the marbled Italianate floor and giant bowls of burnished bronze showcased opulent arrangements of orchids, hyacinths and lavender.

After checking in, they made their way up to their rooms, which were next door to each other on the fifth floor. Agreeing to rendezvous at 1 p.m. for lunch, they went their separate ways.

Helen dumped her bags on her king-size bed decked out in Egyptian cotton. Her room mirrored the rest of the hotel with its white walls, curtains, bedding and minimalist white furniture. She headed over to the window and took in the view of the vibrant London scene spread out before her. The morning rush had died down and on the street below she could see hip, young media types sauntering leisurely between their hip offices and equally hip coffee shops.

She closed the curtains against the bright spring sunshine, kicked off her Kurt Geiger heels and flaked out on the bed.

*

'God, I love this place!' eulogised Penny when they met in the foyer at lunchtime.

'Me too,' said Helen. 'Did you check out the Cowshed toiletries in the bathroom? The soap is to die for!'

'I know, I've already made inroads into them. Sat in the roll-top bath for an hour with a scented candle. Heavenly.'

'What now? I'm famished.'

'Me too.'

'What I really fancy is an American Hot with extra mushrooms at Pizza Express.' Helen's mouth was watering at the thought of it. 'Dean Street is only ten minutes' walk. Let's head over.'

'Ah,' said Penny, 'sorry to disappoint, but I've arranged to meet Neil, the new director, at my club on Wardour Street.'

Helen's face fell. 'Not work?'

'Honestly, it'll only be for half an hour. He'll fill me in on what's going on and then I won't have to go to the studios.'

Helen didn't look convinced.

'Look, I promise it won't take long – and they do a mean cheese-and-jalapeno burger there. And an even meaner Bloody Mary.'

Helen relented. 'OK, but you're paying, Penny Leighton Productions.'

'It'll be our pleasure.'

*

They strolled leisurely through Seven Dials, stopping to window-shop in the many trendy clothes shops, and were soon on Shaftesbury Avenue heading towards Penny's Club, The House, on Dean Street.

Situated in an elegant Georgian townhouse, the discreet entranceway led to a maze of private meeting rooms, bars, and a restaurant that played host to the great and good of London Medialand. Some of the country's most famous actors, playwrights, directors and journalists were members – and membership was both exclusive and expensive.

As they entered, Helen noticed that Stephen Fry was just leaving. The concierge, who recognised Penny, greeted her like an old friend and ushered them into the main bar area, which was decked out in a cleverly realised shabby-chic style that had probably cost millions. Penny spotted Neil immediately; he was sitting on one of the antique Chesterfield sofas that were dotted around the room. The large informal space was peopled by a fairly equal mix of men and women, some in small groups, others on their own, working on their iPads or MacBook Airs. The room was dominated by a central bar which ran the whole length of it, and adjoining the bar area was a restaurant. Both restaurant and bar were full and buzzing during the busy lunch period.

'Hi, Neil!'

Neil, a handsome blond in his thirties, stood and gave Penny a big hug.

'You remember Helen, my friend from Pendruggan?'

'I don't want to get in your way,' said Helen, 'so I'll go and sit at the bar while you two catch up.'

'Thanks, Helen,' said Penny. 'Hopefully this won't take long – right, Neil?'

Neil gave her a reassuring smile. 'Everything's fine – just need to run a couple of things by you.'

Helen left them to it and headed over to the bar. It was busy, but she could see a couple who were just vacating their seats and she popped herself onto one of them as they departed.

Despite the full bar, she was served immediately by a bright and breezy barman.

'What can I get you?'

'Not sure. What's good today?'

'Depends. What sort of mood you in?'

'Feel like being nice to myself.'

'Then I've got the perfect drink for being nice to yourself – the Ambrosia. Champagne, aged cognac and triple sec, plus a few of my secret ingredients. It's named after the food of the gods – can't get nicer to yourself than that.'

'Sold!'

Helen watched as he artfully filled a cocktail shaker with ice before adding the ingredients and shaking them thoroughly. He poured the contents into a highball glass filled with more ice and topped it up with chilled champagne.

He placed the glass in front of her on a small black napkin. 'A drink fit for a goddess,' he said, giving her a cheeky smile.

'I bet you say that to all the goddesses.' She smiled cheekily back at him.

The drink certainly tasted like Ambrosia and

Helen could feel the last vestiges of her hangover slip away.

She dug around in her bag and fished out her iPad. Logging into her email account she skimmed through the usual junk until she came to a brand-new photo of her granddaughter, Summer, that had been sent to her from her son, Sean. Summer was sitting in the lap of her mother Terri and was holding the soft grey elephant that Helen had bought her for Christmas. Helen had had a long visit from them in the New Year and now they were visiting Terri's family up north. Summer looked completely adorable.

In the email, Sean had written:

Summer's favourite toy now, she won't let it out of her sight. We're calling it Ellie.

How sweet, thought Helen.

Next, she sent Piran an email:

What you doing? I'm sitting in Pen's club. Hugh Laurie's at other end of the bar!

Helen googled Heals' website. Assuming the roof ever got fixed, and if there was any money left in her depleted coffers, she resolved to treat herself to a new rug. Maybe they'd find time to pop down there this afternoon; it wasn't far.

An email from Piran pinged back at her:

Who is Hugh Laurie?

Honestly, thought Helen, you'd have thought he'd been living in a cave for all he knew about popular culture.

Never mind. How is the Roman Fort?

Moments later the reply:

Muddy.

'You're a mine of information, Piran Ambrose,' she muttered under her breath.

It wasn't long before Penny said goodbye to Neil, who was heading back to the dubbing studio, and joined her friend at the bar.

'All's well, which is just what I wanted to hear.'

'Fab. I've checked with the restaurant and they think they can fit us in in ten minutes.'

'Brilliant. Time for a Bloody Mary, I think.'

'Another Ambrosia for you, Goddess?' said the cheeky barman.

'I think goddesses should stick to just one at lunchtime, don't you?'

'You're the boss.'

'Actually, make mine a virgin Bloody Mary, will you? I don't want to push my luck,' said Penny.

No sooner were their drinks served than a waiter from the restaurant came to tell them their table was ready.

Helen was just stooping to collect her bag and coat from her feet when Penny grabbed her arm and hissed urgently, 'Don't move! He might not see us.'

Immediately Helen looked up, her eyes scanning the room. It didn't take her long to understand why Penny was keen not to be seen. But it was too late – they'd been spotted.

Coming towards them, wearing an impeccably tailored Savile Row suit and sporting an expensive hair-weave and a smarmy smile, was Quentin Clarkson. Not only was he the Chairman of TV7 – which meant he held the future of *Mr Tibbs* in his sweaty palms – but he was also Penny's ex and a grade-A slimeball.

'Penny, my dear!' he gushed, oozing insincere charm.

'Quentin, how super!' While Penny's rictus grin did a good impression of politeness as they air-kissed, her eyes as they met Helen's told an entirely different story.

4

'How perfectly marvellous to run into you! I was only saying to Miriam the other day that we really don't see enough of you.'

'Well, Quentin, I'm permanently based in Cornwall now, so I don't get up to town much.'

'Ah yes, I heard that you've buried yourself in some godforsaken backwater.'

'Hardly – it's Pendruggan, Quentin.'

His face was momentarily blank.

'The village where we film the series? *Mr Tibbs*?'

The penny dropped and Quentin gave her an unpleasant smile. 'Oh yes, that's right. It's all coming back to me now. Didn't I hear that you'd gone and married a vicar? Can't be true? Penny Leighton, the ultimate good-time girl? Oh, it's too priceless!'

Penny replied through gritted teeth: 'It suits

me down to the ground. I love being among people who are so sincere. Maybe you should try it sometime?'

'Eh?' Quentin was silenced for a nanosecond before he recovered and turned his attention to Helen. 'Well, now, who's this?'

He took her hand, unbidden, and proceeded to plant a slimy kiss on it.

'Helen Merrifield. We've met before. Years ago . . .' She wanted to add, 'when you had real hair', but resisted the temptation.

'Did we? I feel sure I'd remember someone as charming as you.'

'Well, you're pretty unforgettable yourself,' said Helen, removing her hand; he'd already held onto it far longer than she was comfortable with.

'So tell me,' he turned his attention back to Penny, 'what brings you back from the sticks?'

'I'm only here for a couple of days.'

'Business or pleasure?'

'Er . . .' Penny hesitated. While she was perfectly entitled to a break and her company was independent, she knew that Quentin was likely to be aware of the filming schedule. He wasn't her paymaster, but she didn't want him to think she wasn't putting her back into it.

'Business. Making sure *Mr Tibbs* is better than ever for TV7.'

'Well, that's just perfect! Miriam and I are throwing a drinks party tonight – you simply have to come.'

'Well, I, er . . . not sure . . .' Penny caught Helen's eyes, which were looking at her in alarm.

'Nonsense, I insist! Everyone is coming. Sir Nigel will be there, and Baroness Hardy.' Penny's heart was sinking. Sir Nigel Cameron and Baroness Hardy were co-owners of TV7; their good opinion of her and Penny Leighton Productions really mattered. Schmoozing and glad-handing was an integral part of her job. They had just wrapped the latest series of *Mr Tibbs* and securing a new one was a long way from being a done deal. It wasn't all about ratings and revenues; the goodwill of the board could spell the difference between a new contract and cancellation. The future of *Mr Tibbs* and the jobs of the actors and crew were in her hands. *The buck stops with me*, she thought, resignedly.

Helen, however had other ideas. 'She couldn't possibly, Penny's taking me out to dinner.'

Quentin Clarkson wasn't to be deterred. 'Then you must come along too – I'm sure I can offer something much more tempting than some boring old dinner.' He eyed her suggestively.

'Of course we'll come, Quentin, though we won't be able to stay too long,' conceded Penny, avoiding Helen's furious stare.

'Marvellous! Seven thirty – you know the address.' And with that he kissed them both with damp lips – Helen squirming as his hand reached behind her and stroked the small of her back – and headed off towards the exit.

'What on earth??' exclaimed Helen when he was out of earshot. 'I can't believe you've just thrown away our evening like that?'

'Don't give me a hard time. I have no choice. Everyone is relying on me to bag another series. They'd be heartbroken if I failed – and I'd be in the shit.'

Seeing Penny's glum expression, Helen took pity on her. 'Told you we should have gone to Pizza Express.'

Penny linked arms with her friend. 'Note to self: Do not ignore advice from Helen Merrifield.'

'I still can't believe he used to be your boyfriend.'

'Boy-*fiend*, more like!'

And they enjoyed a snigger as they headed off for lunch.

*

Simon was dog-tired. His day had got off to a bad start when he realised that he should have been giving a talk on the meaning of Easter at Trevay Junior School. Unfortunately, the realisation only hit him when he was in the car, heading in the opposite direction to visit a sick parishioner in one of the hamlets beyond Pendruggan. Having shown up late and flustered for both appointments, his day had managed to get even worse when Susie Small, the local yoga teacher, called him to say that the village hall had been broken into. What with calling the police and waiting for the lock-smith to arrive, Simon had once again found himself being pulled in different directions.

It was dusk by the time he made it home to the vicarage. The clouds in the sky were heavy and ominous. More bad weather had been forecast and the thought of yet another spell of torrential rain and gale-force wind only added to his gloomy mood. He hung his coat on the banister and headed to the kitchen. He was starving, but his heart sank as he opened the fridge and eyed its meagre contents. Normally, Penny would have driven to the shops in Trevay to pick something up or, as it was a Friday night, they might have headed out for a curry. Simon felt a pang. Penny would have known exactly what to say to ease his troubles and take his mind off things. He stared forlornly at the bit of old brie and half a tomato sitting on the fridge shelf. There was also a bowl of leftovers from earlier in the week, but Simon's tired brain couldn't remember what it was and the bowl of reddy-brown mush wasn't giving up its secrets.

Shutting the fridge door, he headed over to the worktop and switched on the kettle. Next to it was a note in Penny's recognisable flamboyant script:

*Left you something in the freezer for every
night I'm away – can't have you starving as
well as drowning! Will be a better vicar's wife
when I get back – promise. Pxx*

Simon smiled, realising he hadn't even noticed
it the previous night before he'd staggered up
to bed, too tired for anything more than a bowl
of soup. Switching the kettle on, he bent down
and opened the freezer. In one of the drawers
was a selection of neatly packaged and labelled
dishes in freezer bags: cottage pie, lasagne, spag
bol and a few pots of rhubarb crumble – his
favourite.

Taking the cottage pie from the freezer he
popped it in the microwave and headed out
to the hallway. On the answering machine,
the little red light was blinking away,
and the LED display indicated that there
were six new messages. He pressed the play
button.

The unmistakable bossy tones of Audrey
Tipton boomed out, filling the hallway:

*Mrs Canter, it's Audrey here. I still haven't
heard back from you regarding the Old People's
Christmas Luncheon. We really must make a*

start on it, you know. I'll expect to hear from you as soon as you get this message. Beep.

The next one was from Margery Winthrop, one of the gaggle of pensioners who volunteered their time to help keep the church spick and span:

Hello, Penny, Margery here. Sorry to bother you but just a gentle reminder that we need to sit down and go through the spring flower rota. Doris is having her veins done and June Pearce is swanning off on a Saga cruise, so you'll need to drum up some more helpers from somewhere. Or will you put yourself down for a few shifts? Anyway, I'll try you again tomorrow. Beep.

The next one was from Emma Scott, Brown Owl of the local Brownies, who spoke in a broad Cornish accent:

Penny, my love, meant to say when I saw you last week that spring 'as sprung – so that must mean it's time to get our bums in gear for the Summer Fête. I've already had a word with Harry the scout leader, but 'e's about as much use as a chocolate teapot! You'll 'ave to organise the lot of us, as usual! Bye, my lovely, speak later in the week.

Apart from a call reminding him of his dental

appointment, all the other messages were in a similar vein: coffee mornings, afternoon tea for the old folks, an outing for the disabled . . . Simon couldn't figure out how Penny was able to fit it all in alongside her full-time job. He felt another pang, this time of guilt. He'd been quite cross with her about her weekend away. Why shouldn't she have a break? If he'd had to deal with this lot, he'd want to run a mile too.

He took his mobile phone out of his pocket. It was a decidedly untrendy and ancient Nokia that had been dropped, thrown and even survived a dip in a cup of tea. He'd have his trusty Nokia over a new-fangled smart phone any day.

Simon saw that he had two texts from Penny and a missed call. He'd been so busy he'd not had a chance to look at his phone all day.

He pulled Penny up from his contacts list and hit the green call button, putting the phone to his ear.

This is Penny Leighton, I can't take your call right now . . .

Simon didn't leave a message. He'd call her later. Tell her he loved her.

After he'd finished his meal, he settled himself down in front of the early evening news. *Ten minutes*, he told himself, *then I'll tackle Sunday's sermon*. Within moments, he was fast asleep.

*

Piran had been looking forward to a few hours' night fishing with his mate Brian. Their usual routine was to take the boat out, crack open a few cans and put the world to rights. But the weather that had been threatening all day had finally broken, and as he drove through Trevay hailstones were bouncing off his battered pickup truck with such force it was like being machine-gunned with walnuts.

He let out a sigh. The weather warnings were dire for shipping and, hardy as he was, there was no way he was taking the boat out in this.

The dig at the Roman fort had been a long slog. The finds that they were turning up were incredible, but the constant battle against the elements was wearing them all down. Now that night-fishing was off the agenda, Piran wanted nothing more than to kick back with a couple of pints of Doom Bar and watch some football.

Having made sure that his little fishing boat was anchored properly in Trevay harbour – it was sure to take a battering tonight – Piran set off for the convenience store, where he planned to get some supplies in. The wind was so strong it was all he could do to open the door of his pickup. Pulling the hood of his waterproofs tighter to his face, he battled through the rain and into the store where he bought eggs, bacon, a wholemeal loaf and a couple of bottles of his favourite Cornish ale. The storm had reached biblical proportions by the time he exited the store, whistling through the narrow streets and pelting him with horizontal rain as he ran for the truck. Juggling his shopping, he struggled to find his car keys in the deep pockets of his waterproof jacket. Fumbling with wet, icy fingertips, he pulled them out, but as he did so, his single door-key was pulled along too. Piran could only watch as it spun in the air, landing with a plop in a giant puddle of rainwater that had pooled beneath his car. Letting his shopping fall, he dropped to his knees and began to scrabble around in the cold, dirty water to find it. His heart sank as his fingers made contact with the wide gaps of the storm drain. His key was gone – swept down into the sewer, never to be retrieved.

He cursed a heartfelt bollocks, retrieved his supplies and climbed back into the pickup. The only other person who had a key to his cottage was Helen, and she was too far away to be useful, but he remembered that Helen always kept a key to her own cottage underneath the flower pot in her front garden. So, grim-faced, he headed in the direction of Gull's Cry.

*

Helen and Penny were pulling up outside an imposing house on one of Kensington's most exclusive streets. They'd spent the afternoon shopping in the West End, but the sheer enjoyment of making random indulgent purchases had been dented by the knowledge that they were compelled to attend Quentin Clarkson's ghastly drinks party.

'I can't think why you went out with him in

the first place. Hasn't he always been a complete and utter plonker?'

Helen looked stunning in a Cos asymmetric dress in midnight blue which highlighted her blue eyes. Penny had gone into power dressing mode and was resplendent in an Alexander McQueen red crêpe dress that set off her blonde hair perfectly.

'Well, yes, a plonker through and through – from birth, I imagine. But underneath all that, he's got quite a fierce business brain. Before he took over, TV7 was the laughing stock of the TV world. It was all tacky game shows and bargain-bucket reality TV. Now they've got some of the hottest shows on television. He was ambitious, so was I. What can I say?'

'Well, rather you than me. The guy gives me the creeps.' Helen shuddered, remembering his hand on her back earlier that day.

'Tell me about it!' Penny lowered her voice as they approached the front door. 'You'll never guess what he used to do when we were having sex?'

'I don't think I want to know.'

'Well . . .'

But Penny never finished what she was going to say, because at that moment the door flew open and standing before them was a vision in beige silk Diane Von Furstenberg.

'Penny, darling!' the vision drawled.

'Miriam. How lovely to see you, I can't believe we've left it for so long.'

Helen noticed that Penny's voice was about an octave higher than normal, which to those in the know was a clear indication that she loathed the woman.

'Do come in – and your little friend, too.' She held out an imperious hand to Helen. 'Miriam Clarkson. I'm Quentin's wife, but you'll probably recognise me from *The Lion's Lair*.'

'Yes, I thought you looked familiar.' Helen offered her hand in return but Miriam Clarkson barely touched it. *The Lion's Lair* was a hugely popular TV show where young entrepreneurs got to spend some time working alongside their business gurus. Miriam Clarkson was one of the 'Lions' and ran a multimillion-pound interior design business whose clients included Roman Abramovich and Richard Branson. She was also notoriously volatile. Helen found this odd, considering Miriam's oft-proclaimed devotion to Eastern mysticism, which she claimed helped her to 'channel the energies' of the luxury properties she was hired to imbue with her trademark style.

In person, she was stick thin, Botoxed to within an inch of her life, and the air around her practically vibrated with a nervous energy that was enough to set your teeth on edge.

Miriam ordered a hired lackey in a crisp white-and-black uniform to take their coats, then they were shown through to an impressive reception room, awash with expensively tasteful furnishings in various shades of beige or taupe.

'Psst.' Helen nudged Penny. She'd remembered where she recognised Miriam from. 'Didn't she used to be your assistant?'

'Yep. That was why Quentin and I split up. Found him shagging her on the floor of his Canary Wharf offices.'

'That's right, it's all coming back to me now!'

'She got her talons into him pretty quickly and used his connections to build up her business. They deserve each other.'

The room was full of small groups of men and women talking, laughing and drinking.

The men all wore what passed for casual in this part of London. Navy or tweed blazers from Hackett with open-necked shirts paired with mismatched chinos in salmon pink or mustard. The women seemed to share the same Knightsbridge hairdresser and wore either Burberry Prorsum or Joseph.

Quentin spotted them immediately and made a beeline for them.

'Penny, darling, so glad you could come!'

'Quentin. I see Miriam has done wonders on your pad.'

'The woman is a genius. Insisted we dug out the basement to create a Turkish hamman. The neighbours all kicked up a stink, as usual, but what Miriam wants, she usually gets! The whole place has just been Feng Shui-ed!'

'Really?' Penny raised a cynical eyebrow.

At that point, a distinguished-looking gent in his early sixties came towards them. He had lively green eyes and an open and honest face. Helen liked him immediately.

'Penny, my dear girl! You look wonderful.'

Penny greeted him warmly with a hug and introduced him to Helen. 'Lovely to see you too, Sir Nigel.'

'We don't often see you on the mean streets of West London,' he said. 'How is Cornish married life treating you?'

'Couldn't be better.'

'I love the place myself. The wife and I have a bolthole in St Agnes. Hope to retire there one of these days when TV7 let me out of their clutches.' He smiled at Helen apologetically. 'Do forgive me, I'm just going to borrow your friend for a few minutes, my dear. Baroness Hardy and I want to pick her brains about something . . .'

Helen gave Penny a look that said *hurry up*, then turned to find that she'd been left in the clutches of Quentin Clarkson.

'Alone at last.' He sidled up to her and placed his hand on her lower back. 'This is a big house, you know. I could take you on a little tour – there are plenty of cosy nooks and crannies that we could explore together.' His fat hand inched towards her bottom.

She was tempted to stand on his elegantly-shod toes, but before she had a chance, Miriam materialised. Her eyes were narrowed. 'What are you two talking about?' she demanded suspiciously.

'Your husband offered to take me on a private tour of the house,' Helen said innocently.

'Oh, did he now?' Miriam Clarkson's eyes narrowed with cold fury.

'Er, the Turkish hamman, darling,' spluttered Quentin. 'I thought our guests might like to see—'

Miriam didn't miss a beat. Taking Helen firmly by the arm, she said loudly, 'Let me introduce you to Camilla and James. They're ordinary people just like you and I'm sure you'll have plenty in common.'

It turned out that Camilla and James both lived in Chiswick and worked for the BBC. For the next hour Helen had to listen to Camilla drone on about house prices, the difficulty in finding a parking space for their 4×4 – which had never seen a muddy field in its life – in their Chiswick street, and how utterly selfish her Ukrainian nanny had turned out to be, asking for time off to visit her dying father in the school holidays.

'I used to live in Chiswick,' Helen said. 'But I sold up and moved to Cornwall a couple of years ago.'

Camilla looked aghast. 'But you must be

kicking yourself? Your house would probably be worth twice as much by now!'

'Quite the opposite,' said Helen. 'It was the best thing I've ever done.' And with that, she excused herself, knowing that if she had stayed with those two tiresome twits for a moment longer she would scream.

Heading out onto the ambiently lit terrace. Helen took out her phone from her bag and called Piran. It went straight to voicemail. She imagined herself there instead of here, with Piran, enjoying a pint or two in the Sail Loft.

Sighing, she put her phone back in her bag and headed into the party again. She tried to catch Penny's eye, but she was in deep conversation with Sir Nigel and the Baroness and didn't notice her.

'Ah, Helen – come and meet Emily. Her son went to the same school as yours, I believe, and he's now doing an MA.' It was Camilla again.

Helen looked at her watch. Any chance of slipping away early was diminishing fast. She grabbed a cocktail and a canapé from a passing waiter and plastered a smile on her face. It was going to be a long evening.

5

It was 9.30 a.m. when Helen presented herself washed and dressed outside Penny's hotel-room door. The two women hadn't left the party until gone eleven the previous night, and by then it was far too late to retrieve their evening. They'd made it back to the hotel and were too exhausted and fed up to face anything more than a quick nightcap at the bar.

The door opened to reveal Penny in her bath robe. Helen immediately went and flopped down on the bed while Penny put the finishing touches to her make-up. Despite being the wrong side of forty, Penny's blonde hair, long legs, fair complexion and not least, her infectious energy, made her seem ten years younger. *Simon was a lucky man*, Helen thought, not for the first time.

'Were we ever as insufferable as that lot last night?' she asked Penny.

'You certainly weren't – but I've a horrible feeling that I might have been.'

'Nonsense! You've never shown the slightest sign of disappearing up your own bum like that lot. I hope I never see Quentin bloody Clarkson again.'

'I've no choice but to see him, unfortunately. But at least I'm a step closer to a new series of *Mr Tibbs*. Sir Nigel loves it – he even hinted we might be offered a long-term deal.'

'Brilliant!' Helen clapped her hands. 'And as a reward for your long-suffering and forbearing friend – i.e.: moi – today, we are going to do exactly what I say!'

'Well, OK, your majesty but it's your turn to pay for lunch.'

'It's a deal!'

*

After a light breakfast in their hotel – porridge with honey for Helen and granola and Greek yogurt for Penny – they set off towards Piccadilly station.

A Cornish Gift

'Where are we going?' Penny asked.

'You'll see!'

As they headed down the escalator, the crowding seemed much worse than they remembered from the old days. *Had London always been this busy?* Helen wondered.

Their journey was a rather cramped and uncomfortable one, but they both enjoyed people-watching. Londoners kept their heads down, usually reading a paper or their Kindles. The tourists chattered loudly and took their time getting on and off the train, irritating the Londoners, who were used to a certain regimented tempo.

'Do you remember when people used to read actual books?' Helen observed.

'You're so twentieth century!'

Eventually, without too many hiccups, they reached their destination: Ladbroke Grove.

'Ah. Revisiting old haunts, are we?'

When Helen lived in London, there had been nothing she liked better than heading down to Portobello Road and rummaging around on the many hundreds of stalls for hidden treasures. You never knew what you might turn up. Helen had, in her time, found an Art

Nouveau mirror from the Morris school; a Clarice Cliff milk jug and even a vivid green Whitefriars vase. Her move to Cornwall had been a new start and she'd jettisoned many of her belongings, but those cherished items still had pride of place in Gull's Cry.

They headed slowly up the Portobello Road. It was heaving with tourists and locals. Fashionable young men and women spilled out of the trendy cafés and funky coffee shops. When Helen had first started going there, all the shops had a distinctly home-made feel. Now high street brands jostled for attention. Gone were the conspicuous shaggy-haired musicians and trustafarians, making way for hordes of rich, successful Londoners.

Stopping at a stall selling crockery, china and bric-a-brac, Helen spotted an adorable honey pot. She picked it up and scrutinised it. No scratches or chips, and looking at the bottom she could see that it was from the Crown Devon factory. It would look lovely on the kitchen windowsill of her cottage.

'How much?' she asked the stallholder.

Despite being surrounded by London's

fashionable set, the trader was definitely old-school.

'Forty quid, love.'

'Eh? That's extortionate!'

'Blame eBay, love, not me. That's the going rate.'

'Rubbish, you could find something like this in the Sue Ryder shop in Trevay for a couple of quid.'

'Look, love, I dunno what the 'ell or where the 'ell this Trevay is, but down the Portobella, it's forty quid.'

He leaned into her confidingly. 'Tell you what, gimme thirty and you've got yerself a bargain.'

Despite knowing she was being ripped off, Helen found herself reaching for her purse and handing the money over. The trader wrapped her little honey pot in a bit of old newspaper and tipped his beanie hat at her.

'Pleasure doing business wiv ya!'

Helen muttered under her breath, 'Bloody shyster.' But she was secretly pleased with her cute pot and wrapped it up in her scarf to make sure it was quite safe.

*

Eventually, after stopping off for Penny to purchase a grey kid leather biker jacket in All Saints, they reached Notting Hill Gate itself. You could tell you were higher up as the wind caught their hair and gave them a windswept appearance.

'There's a farmer's market around here somewhere.' Helen took out her iPhone and Google-mapped their location. 'This way!' They both headed off towards one of the back-streets, soon coming to a car park where a dozen or more stalls were selling their wares. Cheese, cured meats, home-made curry pastes and much more were on sale, and the smell of a hog roast filled their nostrils, making their tummies grumble.

'Oooh look!' exclaimed Penny, pointing to a stall selling Cornish pasties and sausage rolls. 'I could murder one of those!'

They headed over and Penny asked for two Cornish pasties.

'Sure,' answered the friendly girl behind the counter. She was wearing a woolly hat and giant cardy; even though it was April, there was still a chill in the air. She put them in separate bags. 'That's ten pounds, please.'

'What??' Penny spluttered. 'Five pounds each?? Are they filled with gold dust?'

'Sorry. I don't set the prices,' the girl explained apologetically.

Penny handed the money over and then said to Helen incredulously, 'But in Queenie's, they're ninety pence.'

'We're not in Kansas any more, Toto,' Helen informed her.

They munched on their pasties hungrily, but both decided – out of earshot of the nice young girl – that they weren't a patch on Queenie's, with her lovely shorter-than-short pastry and meaty, peppery filling.

'Got any room left?' asked Helen.

'Possibly. What have you got in mind?'

'There's a Pizza Express round the corner.'

'Go on then. That pasty was just an hors d'oeuvre!' And they headed off for a second lunch.

*

After a delicious lunch of shared pizza and dough balls, the two women decided to head back to their hotel. Both were tired after spending all morning on their feet and so they decided to spend the afternoon indulging themselves; Helen had a pedi and a facial while Penny luxuriated in a two-hour full-body citrus wrap with pressure-point massage and scalp treatment. It was bliss and her shoulder was feeling better already.

As Helen was calling the shots, she'd insisted that they spend the evening at their favourite London hang-out, Mortimer's Champagne and Oyster Bar in the heart of Mayfair.

'Where to?' the cabbie asked as they jumped in his sleek black vehicle.

'Upper Grosvenor Street, please,' said Penny.

'Any word from Simon?' Helen asked.

'I've tried to speak to him, but we've missed each other. I had a missed call from him but he didn't leave a message, and there was no answer when I rang back.' Penny looked anxious. 'I hope he's not giving me the silent treatment. I couldn't bear it. Maybe we shouldn't have come.'

'Don't be silly, he's just busy, that's all. I'm sure he'll call.'

'Perhaps you're right. What about Piran?'

Helen let out an irritated sigh. 'Oh, he'll be

completely wrapped up in his beloved Roman fort. I've given up!'

They stared silently out of the window, each with their own thoughts, taking in the Saturday-night crowds thronging the streets. Before long they had reached the exclusive Mayfair street lined with stylish bars and restaurants. They pulled up outside Mortimer's and the first thing that they saw was a rope barrier, behind which was a queue of people waiting to enter the bar.

'Don't seem to remember queuing to get into Mortimer's,' said Penny.

'Nor me. There used to be a nice old gent who opened the door for you – where's he gone?'

In his place were two imposing-looking men in bomber jackets with shaved heads and earpieces. Next to them was a small, fierce young woman wearing a tight-fitting black sequined dress and brandishing a clipboard.

Helen and Penny joined the queue. In front of them was a glittering assortment of young, beautiful people. The women wore the tiniest of dresses and there was plenty of cleavage and midriff on display. *Where are their coats?* Penny wondered.

'Look at her heels!' Helen pointed at a pretty girl in front of them who was teetering on a pair of Louboutins that were at least six inches high.

'Ridiculous,' observed Penny.

The queue was moving quickly and before long they had reached the girl with the clipboard.

'Names?' she demanded.

'I beg your pardon?'

'Your names? I need to check you're on the list,' she snapped, eyeing them both with disdain.

The women looked at each other in bafflement.

'What list?'

'Look,' the woman almost barked at them, 'this is an exclusive club and we can't just let anybody in. If your names are not on my list, then there's no entry.'

At this point Helen was tempted to turn around and head off to the nearest pub, but Penny loved a challenge. Besides, she was damned if she was going to be beaten by this brash and obnoxious young woman. Her animal instincts sparked into action.

'Oh, I think there must be some mistake. I'm Penny Leighton, Head of Penny Leighton Productions? We're got a private table booked. Jemima and Russell are coming – they're on your list, aren't they? And Beatrice and Eugenie? You've got them down too, right?

The girl looked at her list and said uncertainly, 'Well . . . I'm not sure . . .'

'There'll be trouble if they arrive and we're not there. Hey, I'm just thinking – there's something about you. I'm casting for a new reality series set in a London club. You look like exactly the sort of person we're looking for.'

'Really?' She had the girl's attention now. After a moment, weighing things up, she seemed to reach a decision.

'OK, give me your business card.' Penny obliged and the girl popped it onto her clipboard. She nodded to one of the bouncers, who opened up the red-rope gate and let them through.

Once inside, Helen and Penny's jaws hit the floor. The Mortimer's they remembered had epitomised quiet, understated elegance; now all they could see was a throng of people shouting to be heard above the loud music and flashing neon lights.

They looked at each other in dismay. Instead of waiters in black uniforms working the room with calm efficiency, the bar and the tables were being served by thin young women in short miniskirts and low-cut tops.

'Do we even dare have a drink? This place is making me feel really old,' said Helen.

'Come on, we've got this far. Let's have just the one and then we'll bugger off.'

They seated themselves at one of the tables and immediately a scantily clad young woman arrived to take their order.

'What can I get you, ladies?' the girl asked in an Eastern European accent.

'Two glasses of champagne, please,' said Penny.

'Of course.' The girl gave them a friendly smile.

'Can I ask you something?' Penny enquired of the girl. 'What happened to the old Mortimer's? The place is so um . . . different from the last time we came.'

The girl leaned in towards them to make herself heard above the music.

'It was bought out by big Russian businessman. He change everything and make us wear these clothes to attract rich big spenders.'

'Well, it seems to be working.' Penny looked around her at the clientele.

'Sometimes the men take it too far,' the girl continued, 'but the tips are good. I will get you your drinks.'

Within a few minutes she was back. While the bill was extortionate, the champagne was good.

Helen raised the glass to her lips and was just about to toast Penny when the words died on her lips.

'Oh no.'

'What?' Penny turned to see what Helen was looking at. Sitting at a table adjacent to theirs were Helen's ex-husband Gray, and his new girlfriend, the actress Dahlia Darling. Dahlia was of indeterminate age, but had once been the Purdy of her generation. She and Gray had been an item for a while now, having met on the set of *Mr Tibbs* and Helen suspected that her vain, selfish and serially unfaithful ex had got himself more than he bargained for.

Dahlia spotted them first. Grabbing Gray's hand, she headed over to their table. She was charm personified and if she felt any awkward-ness or jealousy at Helen's presence, she was far too regal and professional ever to let on. Helen, for her part, felt nothing but joy that Gray was now somebody else's problem.

'Darlings!!' Dhalia greeted them effusively and demanded that the waitress bring them more champagne.

Gray gave them both a hug and Helen was sure he held her for longer than was strictly necessary.

'We're meeting my agent and his wife – we're out celebrating because I've just managed to get a cameo in *Downton*!'

'That's thrilling!' said Penny. 'Just make sure that you're free for the next series of *Mr Tibbs* – it wouldn't be the same without you.'

'Don't you worry, my darling. I wouldn't miss it for the world, would I, Gray?' Dahlia threw herself at his neck and gave him a fulsome kiss on the cheek. As she did so, he pointedly locked eyes with Helen and threw her one of his 'puppy-dog left out in the rain' looks that she knew so well.

They chatted, laughed and shared old jokes, enjoying Dahlia's anecdotes despite the noisy surroundings. After a while Helen excused herself to go downstairs to the Ladies. There were mirrors everywhere and she felt like Alice in Wonderland as she was assailed by vision after vision of herself reflected into infinity. Disconcertingly, when she sat down on the toilet seat she was horrified to see herself reflected mid-wee. *Whoever thought this was a good idea?* she wondered, and deduced that it was bound to be a man.

Heading towards the stairs, she hoped that they would be able to leave soon. They had a table booked at Chez Walter and she was finding the club and the company of Gray and Dahlia rather wearing. She thought longingly of Pendruggan.

As she reached the stairwell, her heart sank as she saw Gray heading down the stairs towards her.

'Helen, darling, you look ravishing. How are you, you look a bit sad – are you?'

'No, Gray, you're projecting – I'm perfectly happy, thank you!'

'I don't believe you. I've done nothing but dream about you for months. How could you throw something so good away? Come on, Helen, you know how good we were together.'

He took her hand and moved as close to her

as he could in the confined space of the stairwell. His face was inches from hers.

'The grass not so green on the other side, Gray? The only person who threw anything away was you. You didn't seem to want the vow of fidelity, but I can honestly say that I've never been happier – you did me a favour! I wish you and Dahlia well – you make a lovely couple!'

And with that, she extricated herself from his clutches and tripped back up the stairs.

'Come on, Penny, it's time to go,' she said when she reached their table, interrupting Penny mid-flow. 'We've got a date with a man called Walter. Dahlia, remind Gray it's Sean's birthday next week, won't you!'

'Hold your horses!' Penny downed the rest of her Bollinger and sprinted out after Helen into the night.

6

It was Sunday. They'd treated themselves to a fry-up for breakfast before heading off to Paddington to catch their train. Not a sleeper this time, and they had a five-hour journey ahead of them, but they'd stocked up with the Sunday papers and plenty of Haribos and had now ensconced themselves in First Class.

'I can't believe we managed to run into all those people. You know, the ones we'd rather not see.'

'Well, they do call it London Village. It's worse than Pendruggan!'

'I'm glad we're going back. I'm not sure London is quite what I remembered,' said Helen. 'Perhaps we're not really Londoners any more?'

'But they say that when a woman is tired of London, she's tired of life.'

'Well, I never heard anyone in Cornwall say that,' Helen responded.

'But we're not really Cornish – and we never will be. Look at Queenie: she's lived in Pendruggan for five decades and they *still* think of her as an outsider.'

'That's probably because she still sounds like a Billingsgate fishwife!'

'True!' laughed Penny.

'I hate to ask, but did you hear from Simon yet?'

Penny looked apprehensive. 'No. Today's impossible because he'll be conducting services all day. I'm afraid even if he could get to the phone he wouldn't call. He's still peeved with me.'

'I'm sure he isn't. Simon isn't one to harbour resentments,' Helen reassured her.

'Perhaps not. But maybe he was right: I should have stayed in Pendruggan and helped out.'

'Everything will be fine. You'll see.'

*

They reached Truro in the late afternoon and the journey back to Pendruggan passed without incident. The bad weather had blown over and the coastline was bathed in a magnificent sunset; the sky ablaze with vivid purple and orange hues.

'Red sky at night,' said Penny.

She dropped Helen at the village green, by the gate to Gull's Cry. They gave each other a big hug.

'Thanks for coming with me,' said Penny sincerely. 'It may not have been the weekend we expected but it has certainly made me appreciate what I've got.'

'I'd have been furious if you'd asked anyone else!'

'You'll be at the blessing of the tower in Trevay on Tuesday?'

'I'll be there with bells on!' Helen joked.

'Very funny!'

Helen pushed the little gate open and waved to Penny. Then she turned to face Gull's Cry.

What she saw almost took her breath away. Outside the cottage, Gasping Bob's wiry brown body was on top of the ladder, fixing some heavy tarpaulin to the roof. He turned around and waved to her from above, making a noise that sounded like one of his 'Ah's'. She waved back at him, delighted that something was finally being done to sort the roof out.

The door of the cottage opened and out came Piran, trowel in hand. His hair was covered in flecks of white plaster and paint.

Despite the risk of denting his reputation as the grumpiest man in Cornwall, Helen threw herself into his arms. He was still *her* grumpiest man in Cornwall, after all.

'Careful now, maid.' He held the dirty trowel away from her, and Helen could tell from the light in his eyes that he was pleased to see her too. 'How was the big smoke?'

'Great,' she answered, rather too quickly. Then her eyes turned to Gasping Bob. 'At last! Something is being done about the leaks. Not that I'm complaining, of course!'

Piran looked sheepish. 'Lost my key last night, had to sleep here.'

Helen smiled. 'Ah . . . Not very nice, is it?'

'Yeah, well. Spent all night bailing out. Sorry, Helen. I was a bit caught up in meself. Should have sorted it before now. But I've repaired the plaster up there, and Bob thinks the roof should be sorted in a couple of days.'

'Good old Bob. He's a sight for sore eyes.' She surveyed Bob's skin-tight shorts and narrow bum. 'Well, he's a sight, anyway.'

332

'Don't let him hear you say that – he's got quite a rep with the ladies.'

Helen laughed and kissed Piran's nose, plaster and all. 'Cornish men! There's no one like you!'

They made their way inside the house and Helen dropped her bags by the door.

'Home sweet home,' she said, meaning every word. 'How are things at the Roman fort?'

'I've got something to show you,' he said.

He went over to his big overcoat and took something out of the pocket. A shy look in his eye, he handed it to Helen. It was something small but quite heavy and wrapped in tissue paper.

'What is it?'

''urry up and open it!' he urged. 'But be careful.'

'All right, all right!' Helen teased open the tissue paper and caught her breath as she saw what lay inside. It was a silver coin, tinged with green and bent and battered at the edges. Helen could tell it was very old but remarkably well-preserved. On the 'heads' side was what appeared to be a Roman head and the words 'Claudius Caesar'.

She looked at Piran quizzically.

'The Roman Emperor, Claudius. We found it a couple of weeks ago. Turn it over.'

On the other side was a depiction of a woman. Helen couldn't make any of the writing out but the woman definitely had a strong Roman nose.

'Who is she?' she asked.

'We think it's Helen of Troy.'

Helen's eyes were like saucers, 'Really?'

'Yep. One of the archaeologists found this and I thought of you.'

'Oh, Piran. It's wonderful. Is this for me?'

'Yes and no. It's now owned by the Crown, but I've spoken to a silversmith in Trevay and she's made you a replica to wear on a necklace. We can pick it up tomorrow.'

'Piran Ambrose, I think that is the single most romantic thing any man has ever done for me.'

'Well,' he smiled, his eyes twinkling. 'Just keep it to yourself.'

*

The great and the good of Trevay and Pendruggan had turned out in force to see the blessing of the new bell tower. Penny and Helen, who hadn't seen each other since their return on Sunday evening, shuffled along one of the rows near the front. Simon had already taken his place next to Louise, the outgoing vicar. The bishop, fresh from his retreat, would be officiating at today's ceremony.

As she sat down, Penny caught the eye of Audrey Tipton in the next row, who gave her a stiff nod of the head.

'She's still miffed about the Great Pendruggan Bake-Off. Queenie reckons that we're the odds-on favourites to win!' she whispered, gleefully.

'Never mind that, how are things at home? Simon?'

'Shush, the bishop's about to speak.'

The bishop welcomed them all and then, after a short prayer, addressed the congregation.

'It's a pleasure to be here today to bless this wonderful new bell tower. The builders have done an excellent job and I'm sure I speak for us all when I say that Simon here has moved heaven and earth to make sure that everything ran on time and on budget, all while trying to run his own ministry as well as keeping everything afloat here. I think we owe him a big thank you.'

The gathered parishioners gave Simon a round of warm applause and the bishop encouraged him to step up to the dais and say a few words. After thanking the verger and the army of helpers who had turned out to lend a hand, he addressed his wife.

'I just want to say how much I owe to my wife, Penny. She's the one who gives me all the love and support I need to carry out my duties. She's the one who really should get a round of applause.' The parishioners clapped her heartily and Penny blushed as Simon said, 'Thank you, Penny. I'm so glad to have you home.' His eyes shone with love for her.

The bishop said another short prayer of blessing, and across Trevay – from the church all the way to the Pavilions Theatre near the harbour – the bells rang out crisp and clear throughout the town.

A shaft of light filtered through the stained-glass windows and shone down on the happy group of friends, Helen of Troy glimmering in its dappled sunshine.

Fern's Favourite Cornish Christmas Markets

Cornwall is a magical place all year round but come Christmas it's extra special. And there's nothing I love more than visiting the local Christmas markets to either treat myself to a little piece of Cornwall, or discover the perfect artisan Christmas gifts for my friends and family, with a warming mug of mulled wine in hand.

So, I say avoid the department stores if you can and head to one of these gorgeous markets for handmade and locally sourced items, delicious food, from mince pies to a proper Cornish pasty, of course, Christmas carols sung by local choirs and all under a blanket of twinkling fairy lights.

These are my favourite markets – and I hope they will be yours too…

Made in Cornwall Christmas Fair, Truro

This is a wonderful market to start at, and one of the most popular. The 'Made in Cornwall' logo is only awarded to businesses that have products exclusively made in Cornwall – so you know you're in for an authentic Cornish treat. You'll find presents for everyone from delicious gourmet hampers to stunning, handcrafted jewellery and wonderful arts and crafts.

Padstow Christmas Festival

Padstow is such a beautiful place and this market really showcases the stunning waterside-setting – a Cornish Winter Wonderland! It's a real foodie favourite with top local chefs, including the wonderful Rick Stein, putting on live cooking demonstrations and the food on offer is mouth-wateringly delicious. I've even been known to put in an appearance for a Ready, Steady, Cook reunion! There's also a Santa's grotto for your little ones, carols and even fireworks.

Flambards Christmas Craft Fayre

Flambards Christmas Fayre features local crafters and businesses all showcasing their wares. The family-friendly fayre has such a lovely Christmassy feel about it, especially as it's set in such a unique location – on the cobbled streets of the indoor Victorian Village, Britain in the Blitz, and Flambards' bespoke entertainment venue. This year you'll even be able to pick up your Christmas tree there!

Create Christmas Craft Fair – Newquay

The Bedruthan Hotel & Spa is the lovely setting for this arts and crafts weekend. This very excitingly focuses on how you can create a magical Christmas yourself, offering workshops on all sorts from tree decorations to make your own wrapping paper, gift bags and cards.

The Castle Christmas Food Fayre – Bude

The atmosphere at this Christmas food fayre is so charming, especially as it's set in a castle. Nothing beats Christmas in a Castle! Find your perfect present from a wide variety of local businesses in attendance.

Fowey Christmas Market

Fowey is one of the county's most picturesque harbour towns and it really does put on a stunning Christmas market. There's also a delicious riverfront barbecue, a magical lantern procession and lots of wonderful, unique sellers offering a wide variety of gifts amongst marquees on the quay and Fowey Leisure Centre. It's fabulous!

Heartlands Christmas Market Weekend – Camborne

This charming market excitingly features 'special snow' and 'enough snowballs to have a truly amazing snowball fight', alongside local choirs and brass bands providing a very festive soundtrack to your shopping spree. There's also beautiful artwork, jewellery, foodie treats and plenty more arts and crafts to ensure all your Christmas gifting needs are met!

Happy Christmas shopping!

Fern Britton: questions for the author

1. What is your favourite part of writing?

Apart from typing 'The End' (ha!), I love it when the first idea of a book begins to form in my head. Then the characters come – some very clear, others a little less distinct, but I can hear them all and it's like they are old friends.

2. Do you have a favourite place to write?

Usually, in my box room office upstairs but if we're lucky enough to have a gorgeous hot summer like the one just past, I have created a cool and shady spot in the garden to write in.

3. What do you do if you feel you need some inspiration?

I put it to the back of my mind and either go for a walk or do the ironing or watch Coronation Street. Anything that takes my mind off the subject, and then the solution comes into my head.

4. When is your favourite part of the day?

Either early morning or late afternoon. The house is quiet and settled then.

5. What are your favourite types of character to write?

I like all of them. The baddies and the goodies. However, I have discovered that no one is either all bad or all good so they are the most complex ones – and the most fun to write.

6. Did you always want to be a writer?

To be honest, no. I had no idea that it was in my future but now I really do love it.

7. Where is your favourite place to spend Christmas?

Home. Always home!

8. Winter in Cornwall can be very cold but also beautiful-what is your favourite thing to do on a Cornish winter's day?

Bang a roast in the oven and take the dogs for a walk on the cliff with Phil. Then come home, light the fire and chill.

9. There's something very English about swimming in our cold English waters- do you swim in the sea when down in Cornwall?

I am a sea swimmer though I'm a bit of a wuss getting into cold water... it takes me a few minutes, but then the pleasure of swimming out in the deep is enormous. Either that or bouncing about in the big waves.

10. What is your top tip for staying focussed when writing?

Give your self a sharper deadline than your editor's!

11. Do you ever go off with a note pad and pen and jot down ideas away from your computer? Or do you prefer to type up all of your notes as you go?

I do like to get chapter shapes in place so that I know where the story is going, but I'm also lucky my editor has sat at my kitchen table and really corralled my ideas.

12. Do you base the places in your novels on places you've been, or do you often write about places that you wish existed- little Cornish villages that you hope do discover, beaches that miraculously have fantastic surf, lovely sand and no people...?

A bit of both! I have lived on and off in Cornwall since 1980 and the villages I have settled in are small and friendly. Lots of farmers and families. So I write an amalgam of them and other places I love. It means I can make a lot of stuff up to suit the story rather than suddenly give Port Isaac a world class opera house for instance.

There's a Fern for every season…

THE *SUNDAY TIMES* BESTSELLER

Fern Britton

Coming Home

Treat yourself to the perfect
Mother's Day gift
with Fern's new novel

Spring 2018

There are lots of ways to keep up-to-date with all things

Fern Britton

f /officialfernbritton

🐦 @Fern_Britton

www.fern-britton.com